LIFE OF THE VIRGIN MARY

A Tale Retold

by

Irene Tester

SEDGMOOR
BOOKS

First published in 2004 by Sedgmoor Books
33 Prospect Way
Lapford, Crediton
EX17 6QB

Distributed by Gazelle Book Services Limited
Hightown, White Cross Mills, South Rd, Lancaster
England LA1 4XS

British Library Cataloguing in Publication Data
A catalogue record for this book is available from the British Library

ISBN 0-9544647-1-0

Typeset by Amolibros, Milverton, Somerset
This book production has been managed by Amolibros
Printed and bound by T J International Ltd, Padstow,
Cornwall, UK

Contents

Book I

The Birth of Jesus

1

The Lost Sheep

IN THAT JEWISH household on the hills above Nazareth, the evening prayers would soon be over. The father was a deeply religious man. He made no move to break the Sabbath silence when there was a noise outside of an animal in some kind of distress. The two sons waited for a lead from their father. Should help go to the animal in distress? A valuable animal. Was this a time to break the law of not working during the Sabbath? They waited. Their younger sister, Mary, had no such hesitation. An animal needed help—she went straight out. She came back and fetched Benjamin. Once all was quiet, they both came back to the prayers.

The time of prayer finished, the father turned to questioning Benjamin. It was clearly Mary who had broken the time of prayer, but one did not question Mary on matters of religion.

Such was a not unusual Sabbath evening. Life on an upland hill farm was hard, even as it is today. This particular household was well run, with three offspring as well as the father, all needed for the tasks involved. The death of the mother left the household doubly dependent on their own efforts. The oldest was Reuben—Reuben aged nineteen, with a damaged shoulder. The younger members were Benjamin Johnathan, aged seventeen, and Mary, fourteen. All were part of the Nazarene community.

For Benjamin, it looked as if the future would make him rather than Reuben the head of that household. He was conscious of this and he was increasingly glad of the help he had from his younger sister Mary. Their mother had died when Mary was nine. With no other women in the family, Mary did as her older brothers did. In fact, she was their equal, out in all weathers and distances, as they ventured out after missing sheep. Interestingly, noted Benjamin, Mary seemed to think even of sheep as individuals. Where had that missing ram gone? And how Mary had followed him. Mary even had names for some of them, and seemed to know where to go to find them.

She also seemed to notice things in a different way from him. Had he noticed that tree? Well he had seen it, of course, but he had not noticed its peculiar shape, or wondered what law it had followed. Had he heard the wind? Yes, he had. But all it said to him was that rain was coming.

On this particular evening, the animals were safely pastured, the family home, and a welcome ready for any visitors. It was true that the most likely one was Joseph who lived with his widowed mother in Nazareth.

To the men, helping an animal on the Sabbath might have constituted work; the father would have needed time to reflect. Whether to break the Sabbath? Or not to break the Sabbath, and thus risk harm to a valuable asset? The two young men had waited for a lead from their father. Mary, devout and prayerful, the one to whom the Sabbath meant so much, had had no hesitation in going out to see what ailed the beast. And the people round her were ready to give obedience to her clear vision.

The round of toil that filled the next six days did not seem monotonous to the family. Each day brought its own problems, each its own rewards. To the four people who now comprised the family, they were not alone, but part of Nazareth below, away in the distance. Just as they were linked in place with the others, they felt linked in time with those who had gone before. Their mother, lovely dead Hannah, stood beside them; they were one with the whole previous line, of So-and-so who begat So-and-so, back through the centuries. They were part of that Jewish community that had survived slavery in Egypt, exile in Babylon...the list was long. In the world of the Mediterranean, any one tribe or nation could point to a troubled history, an alternation of victory and subjugation. To the Jews, it was clear that their own miraculous survival was the result of their vision of their own supreme God—a jealous God; he demanded sacrifice and in return he gave strength.

Was Mary conscious of this history? There had probably never been a time when she was quite unconscious of it, and it was the background to a life that for her was utterly satisfying. The hills around—places of terror to many—were to her places of beauty and vision. Her life was complete, enriched rather than saddened by the memory of her mother. Her disappointments were when her own appreciation of, say, early morning mist, or some individual animal (like that determined young ram that she called Jacob) was not shared by her brothers. In particular, she would have liked to share these ideas with Benjamin. Benjamin, who was tall and handsome, was the next to her in age, and her nearest companion. Had he marked the colour of the sunlight? Had he noted the particular swish—sh—sh of the wind when it blew from the south? No, Benjamin had not. Had God bent down and spoken to him as the thunder rolled around? No, Benjamin relied on the rest of the family to interpret God, and on the next morning was chiefly concerned about getting on with the rounding-up of distant sheep. It would be a long trek, too far for their older brother Reuben.

Benjamin had never been one to reflect much, like Mary, but he was uttering a real prayer of thankfulness that on that day he would have the help of her resourcefulness in what looked like being a long day's work. He did not think to himself that it was a pity his sister had not been a boy—such a thought would have been entirely foreign to such a family, so conscious of their dependence on the will of God. But he was thankful that in Mary he had such an able partner. He remembered that it was only six months ago that she had been surprised by pariah dogs and had almost driven them off by herself before being rescued by Reuben. Mary's own reaction, on that occasion, had been to grieve for "the poor old dogs who were hungry too", an odd reflection, alien to her time and country. Their father's reaction had been to lay down the limits of where Mary might go alone.

Now, she walked along with her favourite brother, her heart high at the prospect of their venture into the distant hills. Benjamin looked at his sister. To regard her with admiration would hardly have fitted in, but he felt glad to have her with him. He noticed that his little sister was turning into a woman, and reflected that it would soon be human lions and wolves rather than the wild ones that must be feared. In the Jewish community, Mary was safe, but outside that, neither road nor town could be trusted. The Roman soldiers kept some degree of order, except, thought Benjamin, that, for a good-looking girl, they were more dangerous than hordes of wild animals. He thought of the wilful and dashing cousin, called Mary like his sister. *That* Mary had heard a call all right before going off after the glitter of the legions. Not that the village blamed her, for the Jewish world was one to acknowledge the existence of its prostitutes. Benjamin's thoughts slowed him down until he became aware that Mary, his sister Mary, was no longer in sight. "Mary," he called in panic. She danced back into sight. "Benjamin, see…this is where…" and there was some story of a tree in the great wind of a year ago.

The two went on together. No, Benjamin had not seen

the tree. Both realised that in all probability he *had* seen the tree, and just not noticed it. They turned to topics they could both appreciate. Did Mary remember the traders who had come through? Oh yes, and that other group with the camels; a wealthy lot, those men, and plenty of strong arms to protect whatever it was they had on the camels. Then the two men who might have been prophets, and the two rascals who had come along a while after, speaking some strange tongue? Nobody had trusted them. But that other little lot, with a couple of asses…?

Mary had liked them, though they also spoke some strange tongue. Mary, unlike the rest of her little world, had a fondness even for donkeys, beasts of burden to everyone else, expected to have no more feeling than a piece of wood. Benjamin and Mary chatted over some of the events of the last year. Judea was one of the crossing places of that world, and there was no lack of all kind of passing trade and travellers.

Was Mary looking forward to the time when it would be possible for her to go up to Jerusalem? Reuben had already been. Hannah had often told Mary about the Passover, the great highlight of the year for a traditionally religious Jewish family. And what family at that time was not traditionally religious? A wealthier family would have servants who could be left looking after animals and possessions, but for Mary's family, without servants or prospect of servants, someone must be found to be left in charge. Mary's face was already alight and happy. At the mention of Jerusalem, she halted. Ah, Jerusalem. There was a quiet awe in her voice as she spoke of it. The time would come when it would be right for her to be one of the ones who went.

Mary touched his arm, and turned her head to listen. "Wait," she commanded. "Wait here." She ran up the slope to the left. ("Moves as if she was a mountain goat," came into her brother's mind). Then she waved him to come on. She was right of course. She had all the time been working out where the sheep might have gone ("silly" sheep did not apply to the flocks of Galilee); she had heard the faintest sound on the breeze, and now spotted the leading ram. The rest was fairly easy, but the afternoon was nearly over by the time they had cornered all the animals and set out on the journey back. Unlike Benjamin, Mary had names for the different sheep, and knew which ones must be caught to give a lead to the rest. That determined little ram, who had given more trouble than all the rest, but would lead his flock home, that was Jacob. Finally, the sheep, the girl and the young man moved steadily homewards.

A quiet afternoon? A strenuous afternoon? Certainly an afternoon in which Mary, unnoticed, had walked and run distances that only strong young men would have wanted to tackle.

2

The Good Samaritan

ABOUT THIS TIME occurred the incident of the "wounded man", which was to be remembered by many more than Mary's family. (Her account, as was that about that "poor mangy old lion", was something very different from anyone else's.) There were many who pointed out that the whole event should never have taken place. Certainly, it could only have happened in the absence of many of the elders of the community, who had gone up to Jerusalem for the Passover. Mary's father was one who had gone. He had left the farm in the care of the three young ones, assisted, as often, by Joseph, a carpenter from Nazareth.

Nobody could say afterwards how it had transpired. There are of course in any community those who are ill-natured, and the ill-natured were beginning to look askance at Mary. It was acknowledged by all that the father was a most virtuous man, and the family upright and hard-working, on the whole, but why was it, one asked, that Mary was often to be seen wandering far away on the hills? She was looking after the sheep, or for the sheep. Or was she? If she did have companions, which was not often, it would be *young men*. The ill-natured, and those who just liked a gossip, were ready to ignore the fact that Mary was the only girl who could manage such distances. Whispers went round. Was it only words and visions that were coming to her in the hills? Was she really communing with God? Some people started remembering that other Mary, who had gone away when a Roman legion went.

Somehow, the idea had taken shape that there should be a round-the-hills race. A *race* (Joseph's voice would be almost contemptuous when he told the story afterwards) as if Jews were like the Greeks, to delight in competition to show the prowess of the body, or Romans, who would do anything if the reward was great. And what made the whole thing worse was that it was designed to show if Mary really could run as fast as the boys and the young men. This would be the proof; either she was an exceptionally worshipful member of the community, and her wanderings were blessed and holy, and she was only with boys and young men because she was their physical equal in so much. In that case, she would finish among the leaders. Or else…the race would show.

The course for the race was arranged. It would end

with a straight run of about a mile, from where the competitors (*competitors*) would emerge from a wooded and rocky defile. Nazareth was only a small place, and many people gathered to see what would happen. Mary's brother Benjamin, from whom the whole point of the race had been concealed, was there; so was Joseph, to whom it had been made abundantly clear. The spectators waited, chattering a little. There was an unhealthy excitement.

Suddenly, the first runner appeared. A shout went up. It was a boy called Matthew, closely followed by one James. There was no one else in sight. Matthew finished first. There were questions; had they seen Mary? The boys seemed embarrassed. Yes, they had seen her: she was back in the wood. Was she running? No, no. Had she fallen? Oh no. Someone congratulated Matthew. People huddled together. They were tense, waiting, silent now.

It seemed an age. Then two more appeared out of the defile. Two boys. Then, at last, Mary. A sort of sigh went round. Mary passed the boys, at a speed that should have brought her in along with Matthew. Suddenly it was seen—one could imagine the shock—that Mary's shift was torn, and there was a stain of blood. Although nobody actually used the words "deflowered virgin", it was obvious what was being thought. Mary came up, to go straight to the oldest man there.

"Rabboni," she addressed him. He was not the Rabbi, but what she had to say needed attention. "We must send help. There is a man back in the defile, who has been set on by thieves and badly hurt. I have torn off part of my garment to stop the blood. But help must be sent."

Matthew and James, the "winners", were questioned. Yes, Matthew had heard the man call. Everyone knew that Matthew would have been more anxious to win than to turn aside to help some stranger. And James? Oh yes, he had seen the man, but he had been afraid; it might have been a trick to lure him away from the path. The older people, including Joseph, then sent to succour the wounded man. Mary, satisfied that help was going, took herself off to her own home.

The story she told her father on his return from the Passover was very simple. There was a poor wounded man, in the defile yonder. She had heard him call, staunched the blood flowing from his wounds, and then asked the community to send help. And how glad she was to see her father and to hear about the Passover. To her father the story seemed a portent. The word of God, which came to most through wrestling in prayer, seemed to come direct to Mary. It was so simple. Help was needed and you gave it. He pondered long. Might the Lord protect her in the paths where this would lead her! He thought about the Passover. He tried to put away from himself the thought that sometimes in Jerusalem there was more magnificence than true worship. He told Mary about his customary visit to Zechariah and Elizabeth. Zechariah was old now, a priest of high repute, and famed for his eloquence. Elizabeth, cousin to the dead Hannah, was a beautiful woman. It was so sad that they were childless, and the years passing. The Lord seemed to act with less than fairness sometimes, for here surely were two who should have been rewarded with issue.

He looked reflectively at Mary. She was not as beautiful

as her mother had been. Well, how could she be, being his child as well? He grinned to himself, and started thinking practical things about sheep.

3

The Roman Captain

A FEW DAYS later, someone arrived from the village. Ah, Joseph, the carpenter, a welcome visitor. But what brought Joseph here on what was surely a working day? As if all days, except the Sabbath, were not working days. Joseph was a little older than the other three. Food and drink were produced, and Joseph seated himself. He explained. The stranger that Mary had rescued, wounded, from the defile? The father nodded. The man had been brought into the village, had been cared for and had recovered and departed. The village had reported the incident to the authorities. The stranger's story was not at all clear, and now there was to be an investigation. "A Roman patrol has come," explained Joseph. "They are going to come on here. I came on ahead, to warn—to warn

Mary. They stopped in Nazareth but they will soon be here. And they have horses—there is a captain, as well as his aide with the men, so two horses which will need water."

This was unwelcome news. Although many of the Romans were exemplary in their dealings with the Jews, one was always uneasy about the prospect of a visit. Their customs took some understanding (a thought held equally by Jew and Roman) and, the Jews being a subject people, most of them had the feeling that the Romans were strangers with no business there. On the farm too, there was plenty of work to do without having to go into official investigations, and start using extra water.

There was no need to summon the family in order to meet Joseph. Arrivals were marked by every living thing, including a distant vulture. Mary arrived first. "Ah, Joseph." Joseph was a dear friend. He had time to stand and observe. Mary, with her visions born in the distant hills, found him more congenial that many of the other young people. What brought Joseph there? Joseph explained again. He told of the imminent arrival of the Romans, who would be wanting to know more about the wounded man that Mary had helped.

Mary received the news with little concern. It would be up to Father to give a welcome to strangers, even Roman soldiers. She must go out again, to get as much work done as possible before she might be interrupted.

The little squad of Romans arrived. The Captain (Captain indeed—it must be something that the Romans thought was important) was met by Mary's father. Captain Metellus believed in treating the Jews with every sign of courtesy—funny lot, the Jews! All right if you didn't intrude on the way they treated their God, Jehovah they called him. His own men, like most of the soldiers, worshipped Mithras, and he himself made a point of showing the correct attitude of worship for the Emperor. He dismounted in front of the older man.

"Greetings, worthy patriarch. My errand here can be brief. We would know more about that man who was wounded and we heard that it was your son who found him. We now want your son to come with us to show us the exact place and how it happened. Your son showed courage, and Rome does not forget."

The account reaching Metellus had stated, "The wounded terrorist was found by a young Jew," and it was a considerable surprise to him when Mary was called. Metellus had intended that the boy, who must certainly be strong and fit, should run behind while he and the aide rode. He looked at Mary with feelings far removed from duty. This was a predicament; he could hardly ride along with a *girl* running after them, as if she was demanding retribution for something, and particularly a girl like this, standing there straight and erect. Metellus had long experience in appraising the girls of "subject" races. Although this girl was not exactly pretty, he found himself wishing he were back among wilder tribes, where he could simply have paid something, then taken the girl up on to his horse and ridden off with her. What had been a predicament now presented itself clearly to him as an opportunity. Of course, his aide must dismount, and the girl could then be put up on the horse, and ride with him. No need for anyone else to come too.

The atmosphere became tense, charged. To Joseph, it felt again like the start of the race. It was not right for Mary to be put in such a position. Benjamin and Reuben had arrived, and not one had missed the way Metellus looked at Mary. But what could one do? It was putting a lot on her innocence and good sense.

The aide dismounted. Metellus watched with some surprise as Mary first went round to the horse's head to speak gently, pat the shoulders, and hold out her hand with a few grains of corn. Then she asked a soldier to lead the horse over to a large stone. Again a few words to the horse, and the girl mounted, awkwardly, but without alarming the horse. A capable young woman, as well as a good-looker.

The Captain and Mary made their way to the defile, and halted. Mary suggested moving the horses to a place where they could crop a bush. "This one, here is one they will like." The horses content, she turned and explained what had happened. It had been a race; she had run in, here, from that direction. Two boys were in the race, she explained, and had gone ahead. In what language was the cry, queried Metellus? The girl smiled ruefully. It might have been an Egyptian word originally, or Syriac, but it was now the word that everyone used when they were being attacked, and it had to be used only too often. That was true, thought Metellus, though things were a little better at the moment. So the man had been up here when he was wounded? Or had he been down here, on the path, and then carried up? Mary shook her head. It was hard enough getting up there by yourself, let alone carting anyone with you. So the terrorist had been up there when he had been attacked? Again Mary shook her head. The *man*, she said, and stressed the word "man", must have gone up there with a companion, and the two were probably waiting to rob someone coming later. The politicos, she added, do not attack each other, and up there you could not be surprised by anyone. These were certainly ordinary thieves, and the one at the back had simply set on the other in order to make off with the money they already had. This was how thieves behaved. There was nothing condemnatory in Mary's tone. She was stating a fact. It was a pity, but this was how such people led their lives.

The girl seemed so certain, and matter-of-fact, that Metellus found himself convinced. It rang true, and if this was true, then he had been sent on a wild-goose chase, and could report the incident as closed. One final point, though. It must have been difficult to get up there? Would she please show him? (Crafty Metellus!) Mary got off, handed him the reins, and demonstrated to him the precarious route, climbing easily, in the manner of a hill girl, and sliding down again. So it was true, thought Metellus. And what a girl. What grace. The extremely surprising thought came to him that if he had not got a wife in Rome—but he had, so this must be the prize of a minute. Surely not too difficult.

He smiled at her. "Now, my dear, that's splendid. We have done our little task. What a clever girl you are. And now..."

Mary turned to him trustingly. There was no stone from which she could mount again, so, so as not to have to perturb the horse, would he please lift her up? The whole situation was transformed by the word with which she addressed him, not the formal "Captain" but the familiar local word for "Uncle". It put him a whole generation away, and it turned him into a friend. Selfish, easy-going Metellus found himself, for what was one of the few times in his life, trying to give pleasure to someone else. As they rode back, he tried to tell her things that might help her. She liked the horse; he showed her the right way, at least the Roman way, to hold the reins. Was it dangerous in these hills? She should travel the lower road to the valley, avoiding the usual road, which was going to be used by the legions. What was her family? They need have no fear of the authorities. For Metellus, the journey was all too short. It was as if he had previously been looking through a dark glass, and now saw clearly; he had found the pearl of great price, he was experiencing consideration for another human being, not the passing pleasure of the seduction of one more girl in a soldier's travels.

Their return was greeted with relief by the family, and with half-concealed merriment by the soldiers. So Metellus had not been lucky this time! But Metellus, as they rode away, was thinking something quite different.

4

Espousals

MARY WAS GROWING up and it was not only the father who was thinking of the possibilities of marriages. Marriage, the continuation of the family, the continuation of their own religion—these were the things that mattered. To Reuben there were other things too, including some of the young women in the community. When the harvest drew to its meagre close, then was the time for relaxation. The land could be said to smile, as much as that barren land ever could. Reuben was becoming conscious of his position as the eldest son, the future head of the family. If opportunity offered, he would make his way down to Nazareth, there to visit and consult with his father's older brother.

So the next time that Joseph visited them (it was odd

how soon that happened), it was agreed that Reuben should accompany him back. It was usually better to go in twos.

Joseph returned to his shop and bench. He had been away longer than he intended, enjoying the company at the farm. Reuben went on to his uncle's house. Uncle Amos and family were in slightly easier circumstances than Reuben's father, and welcomed Reuben: "Ah, Reuben, ever welcome. The Lord was unkind when he took Hannah from your father." Reuben sat with Uncle Amos, passing on the family greetings. That done, he explained that he had been thinking that Benjamin and young Mary ought to go again to the Passover; might it be possible that cousins could be found who would manage the farm for them?

Yes, indeed. Amos spoke with approval. It was good when the young ones were ready to take their share of responsibility. The Lord had taken Hannah, and in Reuben and the other two He had given great blessing to the widower.

A bright-eyed young woman came in. This was Rebecca, a distant and comparatively wealthy relative, from the branch of the family living in Capernaum. Rebecca brought in refreshment. Rebecca and Reuben had met before. Rebecca was quite willing to help Auntie, especially when it meant bringing in refreshment to Uncle, and to Reuben.

Most people thought of Rebecca as having dark hair: to Reuben it was as black and glossy as a raven's wing. Perhaps Reuben's desire to talk over family business with Uncle Amos on that particular day had been not unconnected with the knowledge that Rebecca was likely to be visiting. One would have thought that the vultures dropped from the heavens with messages, so soon did even the far-flung members of the community know of arrivals and departures. It occurred to Uncle Amos that there could be a good prospect for his nephew in an alliance with the vivacious but good-hearted Rebecca. For Rebecca too, one could see a better life in his brother's family than the prospects that might be offered, all too readily, elsewhere. Rebecca, he thought, was a good girl, even though you could not help noticing the attention she always attracted. His wife could have told him of an occasion when Rebecca had been locked in, when...ah, well. Yes, something might later on be considered.

And how was Benjamin? A steady young man, Benjamin, interested in work, not likely to get mixed up with the wild young men on the political fringes. Amos thought to himself that there would be little difficulty here in finding a suitable marriage partner. It was a pity that all young men were not so straightforward. Amos's thoughts turned to Mary, kind and lovely, thoughtful, dependable. Not, of course, vivacious like Rebecca, though a girl of some character. She was like her dead mother. Although Mary was known to be a good worker, and a girl of good character, somehow his mind did not dwell easily on the prospect of marriage for her.

He was called to the evening meal. As the family gathered, it was with thankfulness that he offered up the accustomed thanks to God. "Lord, we thank Thee for providing us with due sustenance and shelter, and we thank Thee for the joy of having a united family. May all walk in rightful ways, mindful of Thee, oh Lord. Amen."

Later that evening, after Reuben had departed, Amos heard the young ones chattering. They too were discussing marriage prospects. They dismissed Mary's chances, not unkindly but a little uneasily: "Oh, that one, it would have to be an angel of the Lord for her." Amos found himself wondering where one would find an angel of the Lord, and if found, would he be likely to make a good son-in-law. It would be important only too soon.

It took time for the journey to Jerusalem to be arranged properly. That the younger ones were anxious to go up to the Passover spoke well for their upbringing, for there were some—and he could not help thinking of Rebecca's flashing smile—who would as soon go to Jerusalem when it was *not* the Passover. The ones in his own family who could be entrusted with taking charge of his brother's farm were precisely those serious-minded ones to whom the Passover meant so much. One hesitated about keeping any of the young men away from the Passover.

For Mary's father, this time was a period of companionship with her. The work on the farm was prospering, the two young men as reliable and upright as any father could have wished. When Hannah had died, his greatest anxiety had been for Mary. He now felt increasing thankfulness to the Lord as he saw how Mary was developing. Of his three children, she was the one to whom the family worship meant so much. She had been given an amount of freedom that was unusual for a girl, and now she appeared fearless and self-reliant. No, he thought to himself, she was not *self*-reliant, she was ready to do what she could do to help others, and to help others she put herself in the hands of the Lord. Mary and her father found much in common.

It was a period in which it would have appeared to an outsider that few alterations in the family were occurring. Actually, very important changes were being initiated. Should Rebecca be espoused to Reuben? The enthusiasm of both Rebecca and Reuben for the idea was among the considerations, though not the only one. After all the proper discussions and exchanges, the marriage was agreed, and the ceremonial espousal took place. The young people found it an occasion of mirth and happiness and enjoyment. To the older ones, it was an event carried through with proper dignity and auguring well for the future.

To one person, the celebrations posed something of a problem. Joseph had for long been a friend of the family, and he would have liked to be considered as a son-in-law. The prosperity and success evident in Rebecca's family, even its sheer size, showed up his position all too clearly. Although he now belonged to Nazareth, he had grown up in Bethlehem in his father's home. When his father died at an early age, he had brought his widowed mother back to Nazareth, her birthplace. As a carpenter, he was able to provide an adequate living for the two of them. If Mary could ever be his bride, she would be as comfortably off, in material terms, as in her own family. But would the shop of a carpenter make up for the breadth of the hillside? And how soon could he support a wife and family as well as a widowed mother? When you were unmarried and yet the head of your family, how did you open negotiations for your own marriage?

As so often in a Jewish family, it was an uncle who was ready to help. This was his mother's younger brother, Uncle David, who had indeed helped with the setting up of the carpenter's business. Uncle David first enquired whether Joseph was quite sure of his feelings for Mary. Although Mary was admittedly so kind and hard-working, and also such a healthy-looking girl, Uncle shared the general feeling that in some way Mary was not in the marriage market. Joseph, however, was quite certain. For him, if Mary would ever consent to marry him, this was his future. The approaches were then duly made by Uncle David. The negotiations were strangely unconventional. The father consulted Mary herself. Perhaps this was because he had no wife. Perhaps not. From his point of view, friendly intelligent Joseph, so long a visitor would be a welcome son-in-law, and he hoped that Mary herself would agree. To Mary, Joseph had long been a friend, more welcome as a companion than anyone else outside the family. Marriage, she regarded as something that concerned the family. If her father thought it right for her to be plighted to Joseph, then it was right. The espousal took place, a quiet celebration compared with that for her older brother.

Now that Joseph had become the future son-in-law, it would be right for him to take charge of the farm when the time came for the family to go up to Passover. Uncle Amos hoped that Mary was not looking forward more to the Passover than to anything else.

5

The Happy Journey

TIME CAME FOR the Passover. Joseph could be left in charge of the farm and Benjamin and Mary could go up to Jerusalem with Reuben and their father.

An added reason for going this year was to find out what was happening to Zachariah and Cousin Elizabeth. The priest Zachariah, they had heard, had been struck dumb while conducting a service. There were more rumours than items of news. It was said that he was on the brink of death, or that he was making a recovery, or that an angel had appeared to him. What was certain was that his wife, Elizabeth, had kept herself within doors since Zachariah had been struck dumb. They might not even be at the Passover. News was doubly important.

Reuben, Benjamin, Mary and their father joined one of the parties going up to Jerusalem from Galilee. It was a happy journey. There were years when the weather was treacherous, or families plunged in sorrow for the death of child or parent, or the Romans were hunting for agitators. This was a good year. The previous harvest had been good. Fewer families than usual had been beset by serious illness. For Mary's family, it was a time of rejoicing. It was the first time (and not, they hoped, the last) that the four of them had been away from work together. Mary had not heard her father sing since her mother had died; and now his voice could be heard, a shout of gladness in the morning, a psalm of thanksgiving in the evening. The four were able-bodied, and indeed carried little of their own. They seemed to be where help was needed, Reuben with an arm for an older woman, Mary carrying someone else's burden, joking with a child so that weariness was forgotten. There was laughter and song by day, and awe and reverence in the prayers at evening. For that little while, the group could have been reliving the days of David. How much was due to the infectious happiness of one family? Probably no one noticed, certainly not Mary.

Even the things that could have gone amiss became causes, if not for gladness, then for mirth. There was the swollen stream to be crossed. As if rehearsed, the stronger carried the weaker, and Mary made the crossing several times. At last, only Mary was left on the far side. There was a joking cry of, "Look, Grandma's been left." Grandma indeed! Two cheeky young men waded back and hoisted her up as if she had indeed been a grandma.

For a moment, Reuben and Benjamin were back at the end of the race, or awaiting the return of the Roman officer. Was such a joke seemly? They need not have worried. Mary had not dealt with animals all her life for nothing; she had that intuitive feeling that tells you when a situation is bad. These two young men reminded her of the young ram Jacob. They landed her, and, so that they should not be criticised, she went on with the joke. She was Grandma. It was doubtful if Grandmas would have jumped quite so nimbly on to the boulder, but she had to call for a song to celebrate the "crossing of the great river". Her father? In the merriment of the moment, she struck an attitude and demanded that "our young singer" should sing them a song. Everyone laughed. "Grandma" and "our young singer" indeed! The epithets stuck for the rest of the journey. Mary was "Grandma", and her father was "our young singer" or "the boy singer". The whole party laughed and sang, and the young men danced, like David before the Ark.

The party reached the evening halting place. Little bursts of laughter bubbled up, as the older ones in particular relished the incongruity of the nicknames. Grandma. "Grandma, will you come and help me down with my bundle?" and "young singer", though it was certainly true that he could sing well. Food was produced and shared.

Another party arrived on the way up to Jerusalem, but what a glum party. It was a wealthier one too, to judge from the amount they seemed to be bringing with them. No one, though, was talking much, let alone singing. They all seemed to stay in their tiny groups as they settled to eat, or rather, as the richer ones settled to feast, and the poorer ones to unpack their meagre provisions. Truly a strange, sad group.

Some said afterwards that it was Mary who first noticed the situation. This was a tribute to Grandma's reputation for helping others, but actually no one could have said who first noticed what was happening; it was more as if the spirit of the Galilean group spread. One after another went over to offer food. Their kindness, or perhaps their happiness, altered everything. The richer members of the new party suddenly found themselves opening up their own bundles and handing out their own provisions. Look, there is food and drink in plenty. Here are dates; let the older people have them. Here is wheaten bread; that should be for the younger men, who have the most to carry.

It was one of the second group who offered the evening prayers.

The party would soon be nearing Jerusalem. Traders from the capital coming out from Jerusalem brought news. The incoming party must be careful. Someone had what? Who? Someone had attempted to assassinate Herod? Surely not. Herod had plenty of enemies, even among his own people, but he was very well guarded by the Roman legionaries. Who had dared such a deed? One rumour had it that it was the work of a gang and the next rumour said it had been one man. Whichever was true, the party could now expect much attention from the authorities.

The "boy singer" was at the head of the column, still of cheerful mien. This, ah, this would be the culmination of their journey, of his whole year, his people coming to worship at the great Passover in the Temple. Reuben, who had been to Jerusalem before, was actually feeling greater interest in when they would catch sight of the people from Capernaum. Mary, who was more interested perhaps than anyone else in the coming visit, was at the very rear of the party, as she was talking to two of the children, and showing them the sights of the wayside. John was eight, his sister, six. Several had whispered to each other that young ones like these ought to have been left with relations, or something, not brought along for such a solemn occasion.

The two children had discovered in "Grandma" a most amenable guide. It was nice to hear about boring old Jerusalem from their father or the Rabbi, but it was a lot more fun being with Grandma, because she showed you all sorts of things; the birds and opening flowers and those pretty little lizards. She told you why some of them were important. Those ravens that they had seen back in the hills, they were the kind of bird that had fed the prophet Elisha. If you asked Grandma a serious question too, she didn't just say that you were too young to understand, she tried to answer. John was greatly exercised about whether, when he grew up, he would be a prophet or a shepherd. He asked Grandma how you heard the voice of God. Mary explained that there were different ways. The first, she said, was to listen to your father and your mother, and to the older people around. And sometimes, only this was a lot more difficult, you might feel God had spoken to you through—say the colour of a flower—or a cloud at sunset. But when you were small, you listened. John thought that Grandma made God sound quite friendly. And it would be fun to have the ravens come and feed you. So perhaps he would be a prophet. He was about to announce his decision when he thought of what ravens *ate*: perhaps he would stick to being a shepherd. He would be a shepherd. He stopped quite still, so that they could hear him announce this important decision.

Like many another speaker, John was about to lose the attention of part of his audience. Violence and evil were never very distant in that country and that century. As they waited for John to speak, Mary heard a faint but unmistakable moan and she was certain she could smell blood, and over there was a ruined shelter giving concealment. Dear Lord, not another wounded man.

John made his solemn announcement: "I am going to be a shepherd when I grow up."

She would have to go and investigate. But the children were not to come with her (no need for them to see what she thought she was going to find). The children must go on and catch up the rest of the party. Mary spoke quite impressively. "John," she said, "God wants me to go over there, alone, and He wants you to start being a shepherd and take your sister back to the others."

Unknown to Mary, the party ahead had already been met by soldiers. They were searching for someone, and it did not take much imagination to link this with the rumour that an unknown man had been stopped in an attempt to kill Herod. Two of the soldiers appeared and confronted the children. The younger soldier was brusque. "Now then, what are you two doing here on your own?

Eh?" John replied with great dignity that they were *not* on their own, they were with Grandma. Grandma had gone over there, and told them not to follow her. The soldier was about to follow Grandma, when he found himself being assaulted and punched from behind. The little sister was hitting the soldier's legs as hard as she could, and shouting, "Grandma said we are not to go after her, and *you* mustn't either." Punch, punch.

The older soldier intervened. He had been part of an occupying power long enough to learn one of the cardinal rules...not to get involved in disputes with children, unless you were ready to be involved in disputes with children's parents and in this case apparently with children's grandmothers as well. He laughed, and addressed the children. "Look if we promise not to go after Grandma, will you stop hitting my friend here, and run along and catch up with the others?" The children agreed. After all, Grandma had wanted to go somewhere alone.

The soldiers were not enjoying harrying women and children. The kids reminded the older one of his own two far away in Carthage. He reckoned there was no need to go after an old harridan who had just gone off to relieve herself. They would go along behind the children and make sure they caught up with the rest of that party of bloody pilgrims. If Grandma found the assassin...the soldiers exchanged humourless jests about what was likely to happen to Grandma, provided of course that that particular part of his anatomy had not been damaged. Oh very funny, very funny indeed. They thanked Jupiter, or God, or Mithras, or their stars, that this particular patrol was nearly over, and, with the shadows lengthening, they could get back to Jerusalem. They added a few more soldierly jokes and curses about Herod, about the Jews, about Grandma and the assassin. How they hated this part of their job.

By an extraordinary series of accidents, Mary's mission of mercy was to go unnoticed by the rest of her party. The younger soldier still thought there was something odd, but was glad that his suggestion of going back to search the ruined shelter was overruled. The boy John was taking his shepherding seriously. He knew his family responsibility to his little sister. Just at the minute, the chief thing was not to let her chatter about things that should not be repeated. Grandma had said she had to go somewhere alone, and if you told the other adults, you could be sure that someone would go after her, for, after all, she was only just about grown-up, and the real grown-ups might not know that God had told her to go off alone. The two children marched quietly along with the party.

Their mother watched them with some surprise. Funny the way they were trotting along, so quietly, and the way they kept looking up into the sky. What she did not know was that John was doing a piece of work for God, and that the children were therefore expecting the ravens to arrive.

6

Journeys End in...

THE REST OF the party went ahead and entered Jerusalem without Mary. Officialdom was in confusion. They tried to corral off all the men, who were then searched, in a perfunctory manner, which added to the impatience of all concerned. It was soon discovered that not all the men were present, some still being with the women. Mary's father, Reuben and Benjamin had every reason to assume that Mary was with the women and children, i.e. with those women and children who had not managed to remain with the men. The women were assured by the boy John that Grandma had gone somewhere and was all right. John would have liked a clearer assurance from God that he was saying what God wanted, but he was doing his best to help Grandma, who had clearly been told by God what to do. The children fell asleep. The women assumed that authority had reunited Mary with her own family. Might the blessing of the Lord rest on them all.

Mary, back on the abandoned track, had only too clear an idea of what to expect if she could get to the shelter unobserved. The rumour of an attempted assassination might be true. She had heard the soldiers arrive and managed to stay concealed. If the soldiers were out searching, it might be for whomever was lying wounded in the shelter. This could be the would-be assassin, or some other poor misguided fellow ready to serve the Lord by taking up arms and killing. Might the God of her fathers show mercy, and might she be given strength to do whatever was God's will.

Once the children and. the soldiers had gone, she approached the shelter. Providentially the moaning had ceased. Mary found her way round the tumbledown wall. There, as she had feared, was a man, lying hurt, exhausted, perhaps not fully conscious. The shelter appeared to have been used as a sort of a hide-out. There was a rough bed, coverings, and—thanks be—water. She took water to the man and made him as comfortable as possible. She bent over to hear a feeble whisper. *She must not seek help. Not seek help*. Come morning, come morning, someone…the voice trailed off…someone would come. But would *she* please stay? Not to leave him alone? There was sense in this; the man could not have defended himself from pariah dogs. He was dropping into sleep. The breathing was laboured.

To Mary it seemed that death was approaching. She

prayed the evening prayers of her own home. She was not sure how appropriate they were, but she repeated what her father might even now be saying. "Oh, Lord, we thank Thee for the sustenance Thou hast given us. We thank Thee for the shelter Thou hast provided. We thank Thee for the deliverance from our enemies." Then, thinking that there was a need for a prayer for herself, she added, "Lord, may I be given the grace to know what I may do to help this Thy wounded son, in this night that is dark only with our human sin and error. Amen."

The man dozed again and roused. He slept again, then roused, and, to her great alarm, called aloud. Would Leah come to him please? Leah? It must be his wife. Mary moved over to him.

7

Harbingers

JOHN AWOKE THE next morning with the sun shining on his face. He could hear his mother calling to Mary. "Mary, are the children awake?" He noticed that "Grandma" had gone back to being "Mary" and wondered if he was still a shepherd. He sat up and looked at his little sister, his one sheep, lying asleep. In an excess of brotherly love, he bent over and kissed her, and stroked the locks of her hair. As little sister had not realised her role of sheep, she resented being woken up, and there was a disturbance. By the time it was over, Mary had gone on to find her father. Pity, thought John, now he wouldn't be able to ask her a new question he had thought of since being in Jerusalem—had God stopped speaking to Herod, or had Herod stopped listening? It was with pleasure though that John noticed the doves. He had expected ravens, but doves would do.

Mary rejoiced at being in Jerusalem, with so many of her fellow-countrymen. There were a lot of other people too. She began to wonder if it would be difficult to find her own family, and was glad to come upon a group from Capernaum, all of whom knew her. "Dear cousin, dear sister to be, Rebecca told us you were coming; Reuben was with us but a moment ago." The younger ones trooped along with her, quite glad of an excuse to be seeing Reuben again. It was a merry throng, and a happy occasion. Accompanied by them all, she reached her father. He was glad to see them...his two families, the old one and the new.

She looked anxiously at him. Would he have missed her? Had he been over-fatigued by the journey? She need not have worried. Her father's prayers rang out spontaneously and gladly. The Lord had rewarded him. His seed was like to go on. His young men were with him, true to the faith of their fathers. The Lord had destroyed his enemies and made glad his heart. Blessed be the Lord, preserver of this Thy people.

And there was Benjamin, brother Benjamin, standing at his father's right hand, as he was likely to be for so many years to come. It was not for Benjamin to listen for the voice of the Lord (nor, as Mary, to be ready to hear the Lord's commands in the rushing wind) but he was becoming, with warm and loving certainty, a companion to his father. To Mary he had been a comrade on their passages over the hills. Now, he was coming into manhood as the companion of his father. He did not pretend to understand the visions of his father or his sister, but warmth and loving kindness flowed from him. He would also be a practical one in the family. He knew his flocks and he knew his money and he loved the people he was with. He would never know the individual sheep, as Mary did, and it was only now that he was of an age to have true appreciation of the stature of their father, even to realise that a time would come when the older man might need help and protection. Now they were companions. Mary watched this with almost a motherly smile. Some young women would have felt jealousy, at the thought that Benjamin was changing from being her ally to being her father's chosen companion. And, quite suddenly, she thought of Joseph. Joseph, who had so often been in Jerusalem, he would be able to answer some of her questions. Yes, Joseph. With a sudden lightness of heart, she went away to join the young members of Rebecca's family. But she was looking forward to seeing Joseph again.

Mary's memories of this Passover were coloured by the enthusiasms engendered by the presence of many of Rebecca's family. It was not only Rebecca who had a flashing smile. During this Passover there would be a good deal of laughter and joking, as well as the great moments of reverence. What a lot to see! What a lot even to begin to understand! With every new experience, questions sprang up in Mary's mind, with little chance of asking or finding answers.

The general quietness of the political situation was, unknown to the Jews, almost as much due to Herod as had been the tension of the first evening. Herod, Herod the Bad or Herod the Mad, had summoned most of the senior officers, or anyone concerned with his exalted security. While they were enduring the confusion of being summoned and dismissed, and told to wait, and summoned again, lower ranks were quietly maintaining public order, mostly by keeping out of the way. Things were usually all right if you could leave the Jews to get on with their own worship. The soldier who had first accosted the two children was happily considering the question of where he would be able, in holy Jerusalem, to find the ladies of the town. That they would be there all right, he was sure, even in Jerusalem. Where there were soldiers, there were ladies. He laughed to himself as he thought again of the little Jewish kid who had attacked him—young spitfire. He felt the bruised place on his calf. All the same, what the senior chap had said to him wasn't right; he had *not* wanted to chase after the old grandma to make up for being attacked by the young 'un. It had been a funny incident.

As he reflected on it, the different pieces of a picture fitted together. Yee-e-es. That was why he had not really accepted his senior's perfectly reasonable assessment of the situation. The boy was grown-up enough, surely, to have said "my" grandma, or "our" grandma, not just "Grandma"? As if it had been a special title? And when they got the kids back to the rest of the outfit, why hadn't someone tried to wait for Grandma? The Jews weren't ones to neglect the weaker members of a family. Yes, there *had* been something odd about the whole thing. Having decided why he thought something had been amiss, the soldier turned his thoughts again to the much more entertaining prospect of where he would find the ladies of the town.

The relaxation of tension was welcomed by priest and participant alike. A good Passover, which, for the older ones, brought tears. So often had they failed in their mission. Now, for this brief respite—Lord, we bless Thee for Thy munificence, may our hearts be open to Thee and Thy word. The solemn prayers, the feeling of unity, merely being thus together, families from throughout the country and even further, the sense of being a gathered people—even the young and giddy found themselves drawn into the unforgettable experience of the Passover.

Might the Passover be ever thus—a spiritual experience, and the renewing of family ties with those living far away?

One visit had not taken place. Zachariah and Elizabeth were not in Jerusalem. They were back in their own hill town in Judah. Zachariah, it was said, could still not speak. What an affliction, and what a loss to them all. About Elizabeth, nobody seemed sure, though her health was reported to be good. She kept herself close and withdrawn, and had been heard singing. This surprised Mary's father. Elizabeth to have been heard singing? A disordered mind does strange things. He wondered if it would help Elizabeth to have a visit from Mary, as there was no longer Hannah to go. Only Mary would not want to stay too long away from her flocks, and he could not imagine Elizabeth wanting to scamper round looking for errant lambs. Nor, it was true, would one have thought of Elizabeth singing.

As the Passover drew to its end, the little party, with

Mary's father, bade farewell to the Capernaum group and set off on the homeward journey. It was to be an uneventful journey, though just after leaving the city, they had a brief encounter with Roman soldiers again. The soldiers were coming from the abandoned shelter. They carried a kind of stretcher, on which lay a body, under a covering. One of them had laid his tunic over the face. Benjamin helped to hurry the children by. That had been another wounded man, he thought, and rejoiced that at least this was one that Mary had not been mixed up with.

8

Brief Courtship

THAT YEAR'S PASSOVER was over. Much that had been foreshadowed there would come to pass, as well as a great deal more that was utterly unexpected. There was the happiness of arriving home, one more journey accomplished. There was a quiet happiness for the men as they toiled home up the hill. How fine had been Jerusalem. How welcome was their own home. Blessed are we when the Lord is present with us.

For Mary and Joseph, their meeting was the rising of a golden sun. The quiet years, the earlier friendship, all were merging in this new experience. Joseph's feelings had long been fixed in a love for Mary. He guessed the extent to which friendship and duty had counted in her acceptance of him as her espoused. While he had been in charge of their farm, he had thought continuously of her. A great treasure was being entrusted to him. But he did not want to hold something that was to be worshipped rather than touched. He loved Mary the girl.

He found that he had been worrying unnecessarily. The Mary who came back from this Passover was not only radiant, but also delighted to see *him*. Joseph, Joseph, so much to tell, so much to ask you. In the warmth of their brief embrace, the realisation came to him that the courtship need not be so long as he had feared. The world ahead looked good. Now of course he had to return to his own workshop, where absence had not got his work done, and he had much to do.

There were a surprising number of occasions when a visit could be arranged. The happiness of these. The disappointment was that there were rarely occasions when he could talk with Mary without being interrupted. What had been such a quiet household was being enlivened by the visits managed by Rebecca and her family. "Reuben, you have not met me before. I am Rebecca's cousin." "Benjamin, this is our cousin's husband." "Mary, we will be with you again soon." A time of visiting. For Mary, a time of getting ready for visitors, rather than hours in the hills. For Reuben and Benjamin, often without their sister's help, a time for more than the usual work. For the father, it was with happiness that he thought of the lives developing for his three children, Reuben espoused, Mary espoused, and his own growing partnership with Benjamin. The father would have been slow to attribute any of their success to his own steadfast ways. His wife's dying behest, for him, had been to continue to follow the ways of the Lord. This he had tried faithfully to do, and in return the Lord had blessed his flocks and his herds—and his children.

It must not be thought that no one had any troubling thoughts, slight to others, weighty to the persons concerned. Joseph was aware of his mother's ill-health. Rebecca's mother, pleased enough at the prospect of one son-in-law from this upland farm, wanted to discourage another daughter's glances at Reuben's good-looking younger brother. By the start of the summer too, there was the news from the capital that great and holy Zachariah was still without the power of speech. Poor Zachariah, they all thought. Mary, to herself, added, "Poor Elizabeth."

For Mary, herself, an underlying disquiet persisted. On the first few occasions of being alone with Joseph (and they were brief) she had been glad to ask him some of the questions that Jerusalem had raised in her mind. Joseph, being from Bethlehem and more travelled than Mary's family, knew about the capital. What did he think of the luxury of some of the houses, Jewish houses, in Jerusalem? And the moneychangers and all the vociferous buying and selling. Even in the Temple? Was this right? In the house of the Lord? Ah dear Joseph, how good to be back here, and with you. And your mother? Is she a little better? His mother was no worse, but not better. His visits, more precious than ever to Mary, were more hurried, and the household seemed always be entertaining visitors before she could talk at any length with Joseph.

This left Mary with her real problem. She was entirely aware of what might be involved as the result of that encounter with the dying man in the shelter. She could almost have asked herself the selfsame question that had occurred to young John about Herod—had God stopped speaking to her, or had she stopped listening? It was not her past action that she doubted: that had been in right ordering. It was what to do now that was less clear. As an unmarried daughter, even though espoused, she was still the responsibility of her father. If she was with child, her father should be the first to know, and her father would be the one to offer Joseph release from the promise to marry her. That was clear. But if she was *not* with child, which seemed to her the more likely course of events, she felt that it was in Joseph that she must confide first. Perhaps her father need not know, for his action would be to ascertain that she had acted as she thought was right.

Her duties conflicted. She knew that Joseph's love might prove great enough still to accept her. In that case she must ask him, and that as soon as possible, but if she was with child, that was different, as it then became a family matter; the starting point must be to inform her father, whose place it would then be to make the formal offer of renunciation to Joseph. She drew little peace from praying.

The happy journey and untroubled Passover were followed by a beautiful summer, one to be remembered. Hillsides were green, the flocks flourished. Joseph's all too shortened visits were a pleasure to all, a delight to Mary even in this period of her indecision.

As the time came when Mary became almost certain that she was pregnant, and must tell her father, a mysterious summons arrived for her to go and visit Elizabeth. Zachariah and Elizabeth were understanding people, who knew that journeys cost money. Arrangements were being made, and money sent. As it was known that in some mysterious way, Zachariah had been afflicted at the hand of the Lord, so it would be right for Mary to go as soon as it could be made possible. First of all, Mary told her father that she was with child, and then added that this was no child of Joseph's. To her father, the way of duty was clear, quite clear. He went himself, at once, to find Joseph; Mary must await his return. She sat herself near the entrance to their house, quiet and outwardly serene, inwardly no more than resigned. But it was Joseph, not her father, who came back first. She need not doubt him. Marriage would be arranged immediately; it was to be a marriage that would remain formal only, until after the birth of Mary's child. The courtship was over.

The marriage ceremony took place, and Mary was to depart to visit Elizabeth. It was known, that Mary was pregnant. There were the usual few, the malicious in spirit, who made jeering references to "the angel of the Lord" that had come to her, and what his name was. There were one or two who believed that there had been a miraculous suspension of the ordinary physical laws. To the majority Mary was known for her visions, and *her* visions, unlike so many others, seemed to result in some action of kindness to someone else. This appreciation was the feeling that grew and seemed to pervade the whole community. They felt that they were participating in something that was the visible working of God's will.

Blessed be Mary. Might God's will be done here on earth, as it would be in Heaven.

The home of Zachariah was not distant, nor the journey likely to be too precarious. For Joseph, his long-awaited, long hoped-for marriage with Mary was intended to be treated as an espousal until Mary's time had come and the baby was born, so it was Benjamin who was spared from the family to accompany his sister. All felt that it would not be amiss for Mary to be away and at the comfortable home of Elizabeth for a while.

They set off towards Zachariah's hometown, rejoicing in their time together again. It was long since they had roamed the hills. There had been so much to think about and arrange. Mary was quite unused to being the centre for so much talking and planning. It was pleasant to feel that everything was settled. Now they were free to enjoy the sights of the countryside, the abundant evidence of the goodness of the Lord. The Lord had set them over the animals and the birds, and the fish in the seas. Some things that they saw, or rather that Mary saw and interpreted for herself, were things that Benjamin would not have understood. He had *not* seen the tree, as she had, not heard any "voice" in the thunder. This was now a happy reminder to Mary that there would be a time when she would be with Joseph, to whom these things were not so strange. With Benjamin though there was much to talk about—about their father, about Reuben's coming marriage, about daily work to be done. Yes, work to be done and more now, without Mary to share it. Soon the journey was over, and Benjamin, as soon as Mary was safe in their cousin's house, must get back to the work.

Mary had wondered what awaited her. She was received by servants, which, with Zachariah dumb and perhaps ill, was not surprising. Elizabeth, she was told, would in a very short time be with her. Mary did not know why she had been summoned. No matter. Her father had felt it right for her to come. She sat thinking. There had been so little opportunity lately for quiet, and in these few moments she thought, unexpectedly, not of Joseph, but of the man back in the shelter outside Jerusalem. That poor young man, like Zachariah, like all the Jews, had longed to leave a seed, not to pass away without offspring. She prayed that she might bring this child, unwittingly entrusted to her by a dying man, safely to life. Dear Lord, remain to me a rock and a salvation; may I be steadfast, worthy to be used for Thy purposes.

Her thoughts were interrupted by the entry of Elizabeth. Elizabeth! Dear cousin! Elizabeth—warm, friendly—hands and arms outstretched. Elizabeth—with child. So this, this was the great joy. Mary fell into Elizabeth's arms. Oh Elizabeth—how my mother would have rejoiced. And my father. And all of us. A child to come for thee and Zachariah. Blessed be the Lord. A miracle, a miracle. There were tears, from both of them, rejoicing, cries of gladness.

Elizabeth, homely and radiant, clasped her young cousin in her arms. It was true. With Zachariah stricken in years, and old herself, she was yet to bring a child into the world. Newly perceptive, she looked at Mary. Now it was the turn of Elizabeth, a prescient and prophetic Elizabeth, to utter the words of congratulations—you,

Mary, with child. Blessed be the Lord. Zachariah's child shall be a leader of his people, old though I am. And from you, Mary, in the flower of your youth, shall come one who is greater.

These thoughts had come as a revelation to Elizabeth. Yes, the child so miraculously coming to her and Zachariah in their old age could indeed be destined to be a great prophet. How much more then was Mary's child destined for—for greater things yet. From Mary, young and sound in body, a perceiver already of visions, what might not come? Truly one of greater stature yet. Was the Lord, who had blessed the Jewish people through the years, again bringing forth prophets and leaders for them? The Lord shall bless us and keep us. His face shall shine upon us.

After the outburst of rejoicing, there was time for all the enquiries and the items of news. They sat together in quiet satisfaction. Elizabeth answered Mary's unspoken questions. First of all, she explained that she had been slow to believe in her pregnancy, though Zachariah had been confident. And then it was Zachariah who had insisted on their immediate return to their own home. Jerusalem, and Mary would find this hard to understand, could be a place of danger. Was it not the Holy of holies? Well, yes. Only sometimes men did not listen to the word of God, and then Jerusalem became—Elizabeth was far too happy to say something like "an abomination to the Lord", but her meaning was clear. She made Mary conscious that among the many in their holy city, not all were leading the prayerful lives one would have liked. Why, even the Passover could have its dangers.

The two women sat long together, happy and relaxed. Elizabeth was as jubilant over Mary as she was for herself. And how fine that, on a quiet hillside farm in Galilee, Mary would be having her child safely with her own family, and with her husband. Joseph was he called? Joseph from Bethlehem. Far, far better than in one of the crowded villages round Jerusalem, thronged with Gentiles, and alive with barter.

Mary remained with Elizabeth for the next three months, until Elizabeth's child was born. It was an unexpectedly easy delivery of a fine boy. Mary could not help feeling that Elizabeth's state of happy exaltation had made everything that much easier. When it came to giving the name of the child, Elizabeth unhesitatingly gave the name "John". But no one in the family had that name. Surely Zachariah would have been more suitable, or the name of his father, or his father's father? Zachariah was approached. He signed for them to bring writing materials, then, quite clearly, wrote down in great letters the name "JOHN", just as his wife had said. At that point the power of speech returned to him.

Now Mary had to return to her own home. She felt conscious of a time truly spent in the presence of the Lord. Might his presence remain with her, whether her child was to be born one of the prophets of her people, or, more probably, an ordinary Jewish boy in a loving Jewish home. Blessed be the Lord, who knows the secret ways.

9

Happy Home Coming

JOSEPH WAS TO escort his wife home. He felt that he could not bear to be any longer away from her, and Benjamin had much work to do. Some of this was caused by the necessity for making up for Reuben's mistakes: the family would be glad when Reuben's attention was centred a little less on events in Capernaum and a little more on their own work. So it was good that Joseph could go to fetch Mary. It was felt that it was quite late enough in pregnancy for Mary to be making a journey. Joseph, and his Uncle Samuel, Mary's Uncle Amos and the whole family discussed the question of transporting, and obtained a fine riding donkey. It was a good animal, purchased at the finish by a brother-in-law of Rebecca's mother, who had trading connections. No one really doubted Mary's ability to come on foot, but this should be something special. How they had all missed her. Perhaps her absence had shown up just how much in their daily life depended on her.

So Mary would return on a donkey. In his own heart, Joseph felt that a fine horse would have been more suitable, like that one ridden so long ago by the Roman captain. Or even one of those legendary racing camels belonging to the rulers of the east. As a practical man, Joseph the carpenter was glad to have the donkey. He had no doubt that to Mary it would be an animal of some special sagacity.

Elizabeth would have liked Mary to stay longer, and at the same time was rejoicing that she should now be going back to her own home. It was late enough for journeying. Her thoughts went to the future. How her son would have grown when Mary saw him next—next year, she hoped. And Mary too would be a mother by then, no doubt of a fine child, and cousin to her own John.

It was a glad moment when Joseph arrived at the fine house. There was surprise and excitement over the donkey. Joseph was hardly surprised that the animal seemed immediately to "take to" Mary—he had come to accept Mary's attractiveness to creatures and humans alike. There were farewells to Elizabeth and her household: their final sight of Elizabeth was her retreating back as she hurried away in answer to a cry from the baby.

Mary and Joseph were happy being together again. She listened to all he had to tell her of news from home. Reuben's wedding was to be in the early spring, that was to say, a month or two after Mary and the child had gone to Joseph, and well before the Passover. And who would be going up to the Passover? And how was Benjamin? As reliable as ever? And her father, above all, how was her father? It seemed as if she had been away for much longer, as Joseph recounted the incidents about this one and that, close relations, distant kinsfolk and the people who would soon be Mary's near neighbours. He recalled all these details that he had treasured up to tell her. He felt a great and abiding joy at being again with his bride-to-be, his future wife. As they unfolded their plans for the future, the thought came to him, unbidden, prophetic, as it had done to Mary, of their responsibility for the unborn child. He had felt no special feeling of magnanimity, when he had accepted the unexpected situation: Mary was something special, and he had accepted her pregnancy without demur or vestige of reproach. While making clear that their "marriage" should not start till after the birth of the child, he had been giving little thought to the child itself. Perhaps it was Mary's increasing size (to which he had not been able to accustom himself gradually) that helped to make him think of the child as something separate from Mary. He suddenly realised that to this child he, Joseph, must bear some special relationship. This child would be fatherless, unless he accepted the full responsibility. Whatever happened, this child must be as important as his own. Might the Lord give him such strength as had been given to his own great ancestor, David, son of Jesse, that would ensure that this child should never feel fatherless.

Joseph, Mary and the donkey made a less than

triumphal entry to her home. Everyone was out working. However, in a remarkably short time the family gathered, and immediately it seemed that everyone was bent on doing their utmost to make it a happy time for Mary. People had missed her, and wanted her to know this.

Throughout, the feeling grew in both Joseph and Mary that they had somehow been put into an unusual position—accountability even? That the neighbourhood had accepted Mary's singular status was tribute indeed to her character. It was also a sign that the family and the community were of the opinion that some special provision of the Lord was taking place before them. This then was the background to all their lives in this little period. It was like a background of high hills, in front of which are played out men's little personal dramas. There were many visits, as one and another came to visit Mary, or to see Joseph. Mary's father conducted their Sabbath prayers with quiet jubilation. Reuben brought messages, and presents—a blue cloak, or fine woven wool—from Rebecca's mother. Benjamin smiled as he went about his work, and laughed at the antics of the more unruly of his flock. The sun sank in splendour, the stars glowed in cold, serene skies, and one brighter than usual hung in the south. It was a time of family happiness, each day bringing fresh evidence of gentle care one for another.

One thing that surprised Mary, who laughed afterwards as she told Joseph about it, was a visit from the little boy John, and his questions about Grandpa. Grandpa had said that wood was a living thing, but how could it be, if you had cut down the tree you got it from, and especially if the tree that you had cut down was one that you had had to cut down because it was already dead? What did Grandpa mean? It was not the metaphysics that puzzled Mary, but the reference to Grandpa. Whatever she thought about the tree and life and death, both John's grandfathers were dead, and John himself hardly of an age to feel that they were speaking to him. Then Mary remembered. *She* had been "Grandma", so Joseph would clearly be Grandpa. Although it seemed a long time since that happy journey, when the nickname had been given, the current of life flowed on in the same channels—father, family, ever the expectation of new life to replace the old, her child to fill the place vacant since Hannah's death.

John explained to Mary what it was that Joseph had been making out of the tree that had been cut down. Mary explained to John that when a tree died, a new one might spring up to take its place and while you had something from the old tree, you remembered it. God does not want us to forget things, she reminded him, so she further added, "When you were small, you had to make sure that you went on looking at a lot of new things—when you are older you will have to remember them." John relaxed. That was all right. He was not very good at not forgetting things; and he liked looking at new things. He thought of something he wanted to see with Grandpa, and dashed away.

It was the last afternoon that the little boy was to come up to propound his questions. The fabric of their immediate existence was about to be shattered, not by Herod, but by an edict from imperial Rome. Rome felt that there had been too much unrest, attempts at assassination—even a pro-consul killed. Rome needed more money, and pro-consuls must pay more for the privilege of being allowed to collect it. If they were to gather in more money, there needed to be an up-to-date assessment of how many potential payers could be found in each district. Hence, a new census must be taken. One of the problems facing any far-flung empire is to pinpoint exactly where government can lay hands on the governed; in Judea, the census would be taken where those particular subjects had been born. Joseph, son of the long line stretching back to David, must return to Bethlehem, and Mary, as his legally wedded wife, must go too. The gentle autumn days must give way, metaphorically as well as actually, to winter.

For a young and healthy woman, the journey to Bethlehem, even childbirth, was a source of potential difficulty rather than actual danger. Joseph, one said to another, knows Bethlehem. There will be friends in plenty to take them in, though it would be good if it had been earlier in the year. The family were anxious. But what could one do? It might not be the will of God, but it was the will of the distant Caesar who ruled their lives. All one could do was to help Joseph with the preparations for the journey, as he tried to amass what was necessary, and, unsuccessfully, to hide his worries from Mary. He felt his responsibilities, to her, and to the unborn child. He was partly reassured by her attitude. She was in that state of inward peace that came from putting herself in the hands of the Lord, that Lord who had spoken always when his people had listened. She made the most of the final days. Her father was to think of the guidance he had always given her; great shall be our trust in the Lord, great indeed our rejoicing when a child is born. Reuben, dear Reuben, we shall be back in time for the wedding. Rebecca must tell her mother how glad we are of the warm blue shawl they sent. Benjamin, what times we have had together on the hills; if God wills we shall have more.

To Joseph, Mary turned with every confidence. The donkey would now be important as well as just useful. The time had come, sooner than they had expected, for her to leave her home. But soon they would be back. Everyone hung on those last words. Farewell, farewell. God be with you. We shall see each other again soon.

As they moved out of sight of her home, Mary's final thoughts were of her mother, and what Hannah had said to her, the time that she and Reuben had driven off pariah dogs. "You were a brave girl, Mary, my lambkin; that was because you were protecting something smaller and weaker than yourself, and you knew it was God's purpose; those two things are your shields."

Book II

The Childhood of Jesus

10

Out of the East

IT WAS NOT only Joseph and Mary who were on a journey that would bring them to Bethlehem. At the court of a Persian princeling, the other side of the world as far as Mary's family was concerned, there was an outstanding ruler. Was he, or was he not, a ruler? He ruled under Rome. Rome provided law and order, and the means of enforcement, and on the whole left him to appear to be the ruler. If fire warmed you, you were glad of the warmth, and you did not put your hand in the flames. If Rome said, "Do such-and-such," you accepted that it was theirs to command and you did what was ordered, unless you were a fool and wanted more than your hand destroyed. Within these limitations, there was much individual freedom. Indeed, many little courts of the East, in their hearts, looked down on their Roman overlords. Estimable, practical people, the Romans, but without any real sense of religion or of the inner meaning of life. Throughout the eastern part of the Roman Empire, there was this vast and surging interest in—religion? The interpretation of the world around them? True, impostors thrived on this. Everywhere there were fortune-tellers, magicians, soothsayers. A man telling some tale had a ready audience in any little crowd. On the edge of his audience there would be the usual motley gathering, thieves and pickpockets, and the secret spies for the great of the land, and the simple conjurors, all those who were ready to take advantage of the credulous. And among the credulous were the genuine seekers, those who believed that somehow man lived not by bread alone.

At the courts around the rulers, there gathered the greatest of the wise men. Some were schemers and hypocrites, who had learnt that a holy countenance and downcast eyes meant prospects of a good living. And some were men who truly sought, and sometimes found.

Such were the chief wise men of this Persian princeling. The oldest and wisest was Balthazar. One could have imagined Balthazar worshipping at ease with Mary's father on a Sabbath evening. Actually, Balthazar held the Jews in high esteem; from what he had heard and the little he had seen, he judged them to have made already a spiritual progress denied to even the best of the Egyptians and the Romans. That poor people everywhere, apart from the Jews, had to have various images to worship was not surprising. Like children who have never grown up, they wanted something that outward eyes could see. Balthazar knew the Jewish scriptures. He remembered the story of the wives of Jacob, who had secretly packed their own gods into the baggage. Silly women. Women were like that, though, and it would have been kinder if Jacob, or Jacob's God, had left them their precious toys. Great insight did lie—though not always—with the Jews. Balthazar himself could never envisage a future in which mankind continued to be divided into a selected and favoured minority, namely the Jews, and the rest— namely the Gentiles. But Jews had escaped the great superstition that had engulfed Egypt and Rome, the deification of the leaders, a Pharaoh or a Caesar. From the kingdom of Judea some light might at any time be expected to come to a world that, with all its cruelty and superstition, was seeking a true spiritual awakening.

Melchior, the second of the wise men, was much as Balthazar, perhaps a little less learned, at first sight absent-minded, and certainly more at home with a night sky than a courtier's day. He was of course clothed in fine raiment, but that was only because he dressed himself in whatever was laid out for him by the court servants. On one occasion (a tale that lost little in the re-telling) one courtier had wagered with another that if the servant laid out the prince's crown, Melchior would put it on. A servant was bribed, and one of the prince's crowns purloined and laid out with Melchior's clothes. The court waited. Then—yes—Melchior appeared wearing the crown. How everyone laughed, particularly the courtier who had made the wager. The only one who did not laugh was the Prince, but that was for fear that the jest might have been wounding to Melchior. Not Melchior. He let someone take off the crown, remarked on which particular constellation it resembled, and retired to ponder on what he had seen in the sky the night before. He was often referred to afterwards as "King"; indeed the nickname was often given after that to all three of them. It mattered little to Melchior, who seemed to be unaware of external trappings and would have been equally at home in hovel or palace—provided the welcome was genuine.

The third of the group had been a most unlikely candidate for such an honoured position. His mother had been a lively dancer at the court, with long tossing dark hair and flashing dark eyes—not unlike Reuben's Rebecca. Unlike Rebecca, she had no careful and worshipping family behind her. It was said that she was descended from the Queen of Sheba, a pretty unlikely story, but the kind of thing that was said about that kind of young woman. To be descended from Cleopatra was more probable, but it would have been—well, dangerous—to whisper that. A brief career as dancer at the court had ended in disgrace and death. Her baby (the identity of whose father was in even more doubt than the question of her descent from any queen) grew into a lively merry child and, after a time in the streets, was found a place at the court. It was a surprise to everyone when Balthazar had come forward and chosen the young man to be one of the group of magi gathering at this court.

Balthazar had sensed the concern ever underlying the young man's merry-making. There were jests in plenty, but never at anyone's expense, and children flocked to follow the young man. If "King" Balthazar would have been at peace with Mary's father, this young man would surely have found true companionship in Mary's kindly appreciation of all the things around them.

It was a world that was searching. Again and again it seemed to Balthazar that something might arise among the Jews, some answer. A star, brighter than was usually seen, hung over Jerusalem. The time had come perhaps to travel there. Balthazar and Melchior were perfectly well aware of the astronomical probabilities, and did not think of the star as a heavenly signpost put up for their benefit, but all the same the time might have come for a journey. Inevitably, half the court would then say that they had gone "to follow a star". The prince saw that they were loaded with costly and precious gifts; honour must be done if they met one worthy. Riding camels were selected. Servants and baggage camels were provided, together with all the apparatus for crossing the desert. The journey might he dangerous. It was more likely to be easy, for the fame of the "kings" Balthazar and Melchior was not unknown. In that world, the human ability to wonder often turned into superstition, but true veneration and reverence were often there ready to surface.

The young man was to go too, to be the third of the wise men. The prince was aware of the difficulties they might encounter; wherever this third wise man went, he would know what the children were saying. As the old Jewish writer had it, wisdom sometimes came "out of the mouths of babes and sucklings". Wisdom was not always found in palaces, and the young man might hear things hidden from the other two. Might the three of them be given eyes to see and ears to hear; might they not overlook any new revelation, from whatever unlikely source.

Their journey across the desert was as they had expected it to be, full of interest for those who could notice what was going on around them, deadly dull for any who expected hair-raising adventures. There were many other people approaching Bethlehem and Jerusalem, and the youngest wise man was collecting a fund of new tales. There were stories in plenty, as the Jews and their wives and their children returned to their places of birth for the census. There were comments on the great star, and a few quoted the Jewish prophecy of something great that was to come out of Bethlehem. More were giving warnings about Herod. Something great had come out of him all right, leaving only the dregs. "You don't go to Jerusalem these days without knowing what you are up to." The youngest wise man added these comments to his own impressions. One learnt to discount what one ruler might do in his few years of power; there might yet be some new awakening in a people like the Jews.

The wise men learnt that if they wanted to avoid one particularly crowded place, they had better avoid Bethlehem. With camels, they would hardly be needing water, and it looked as if they were pretty well stocked with provisions, and the small town of Bethlehem was becoming too full for comfort. A few extra miles mattered little to the camels, or an extra day to their riders. They avoided Bethlehem and made for Jerusalem. If there were some new awakening, surely it would be in Jerusalem. They halted outside for the final night. A fair and holy city, Jerusalem, already rich with history, stained indeed with blood in the past. Balthazar gazed at the city. Was there happening there, even now, the birth of some new prophet who could lead a waiting mankind to peace? Or would the fear and cruelty that had tarnished the Jewish past (everyone else's for that matter) again erupt and overcome any new movement? He longed to spread out wings and protect this great city from evil.

Now he must sleep, they must all sleep. Tomorrow might see for them a meeting with someone born to be great. They must be ready. The loads were untied. Camels, wise men and servants rested. Their reputation had gone before them, carried by passing traffickers; they did not even put out watchmen. The third of the wise men, the young man from the streets, slept less well than the others. He noticed that they were in a grove of olive trees.

The next morning, they arose as the first crack of light appeared in the east. Jerusalem, swathed in morning mist, beckoned them. In such a city, they thought, might there be, at this very moment, some new awakening for mankind?

The camels and baggage were to be moved round to the east. It was all very well for the kings, especially that absent-minded Melchior, to be heralding a new dawn. The servants, and perhaps the third "king", also wanted to be ready for any quick retreat. The camels and baggage were moved round to a halting place on the Bethlehem road. Then, along with the folk from the country round, the three kings and two servants entered the city. The third and youngest did not have a servant, for he was not easy with one. It had never seemed right to him that a descendant of a "Queen of Sheba" should himself have servants.

Balthazar was too old and wise to have set undue

importance in advance on any day or experience. He would assuredly have been bitterly disappointed in his pilgrimage through Jerusalem. A holy city? Waiting for some new revelation? It was a city of jostle, more likely to be on the lookout for new bargains. Everywhere men were buying and selling. Gesticulating crowds pushed for place. Women were elbowed aside… "Come on, come on, move over there, can't you?" Priests there were too, amply clad against the cold, and most of them more anxious to show off their own sacred importance than to help some poor woman with a crying child. The wise men moved along with the crowds, and found occasion to ask their questions. Had there been some new birth? Was this why there was such a crowd? There was good-natured laughter at this, and a little jeering. Reverend sirs, it is the census that has brought so many people; in any case it is nearly as crowded as this at any time. Someone added that it was even more crowded at the Passover, and someone else said that that was different. It was the considered opinion of those questioned that if the strangers were looking for something of importance, then there was only one place to go, and that place was the palace of Herod. Some obligingly pointed the way. Others tried to sell amazing bargains to these richly apparelled strangers.

A few picked up the whisper of a new birth, and passed it on. A palace spy knows what to report.

The wise men drew apart from the crowd and conferred together. It had not occurred to them to think of the Courts of Herod. Perhaps they had been wrong; perhaps some new hope might after all spring up in a place as unlikely as the court of the notorious Herod? It became clear that this was where someone must go, and that "someone" would be the Kings Balthazar and Melchior, along with their servants. They would meet again with the youngest at nightfall, with their camels and baggage. It might be that the youngest of them would find other answers, elsewhere.

The youngest wise man did not share their unhappiness about the city. To him, it was a place full of adventure and surprises and above all people. The court in the East had been right in surmising that the young man would be able to learn in places closed to the other two. He started making up a story about someone trying to sell him the Temple. He surveyed the scene in front of him. Not much in the way of new revelations here? His eye was caught by an ill-clad wretch trying to entertain the crowd and extract some money. Poor chap. The wise man had spent enough time on the streets himself to assess such a situation; this was a poor performance and the crowd could easily turn nasty and turn on the performer. He would try to distract their attention. He struck an attitude and yelled, "Good people, great citizens, descendants of Abraham and Isaac and Jacob..." He added a few more names, less well-known, but from the scriptures, "...and of Aminadab and of Aram." He had caught their attention. What could he sell? He pulled out a few sprigs of olive that he had picked at their resting place the previous evening. He made a show of displaying the twigs, though keeping them as much hidden as he could. "Here I have a mysterious plant from my own far country that will give you the chance of everlasting life. See! Everlasting life for you, and many children to your womenfolk." Several voices interrupted him to inform him that these were olive twigs, more likely to be from Gethsemane than any far country. He joined in the laughter against himself, and noticed that the ill-clad one had taken the opportunity to slip away. Good. It seemed a pity though to waste a good audience, whose reactions too might tell him quite a bit about what was happening in Jerusalem. He started again. What could he offer them? An idea came to him. "Worthiest inhabitants of the Roman Empire—I tell you—I could sell you a stone from the great Temple, a stone which would cure an inner sickness—but the greatest treasure of all (and this you know from your priests) is a heart without malice." This did not go down very well. He had hoped that he was echoing what their priests would have told them, but either he or the priests had got the message wrong. He went on: "Great is the holy Temple of your people, the temple built by the masons and carpenters of mighty Solomon, restored by Nehemiah, in the days of Cyrus the king of Persia." He wondered if a flippant reference to descendants of "The Queen of Sheba" would have brought a laugh. No, it was a bit risky when you didn't know your audience. He rambled on, carefully losing the thread of his discourse until the crowd had melted away.

Whither next? He picked up a couple of stones, to start to juggle. It might attract children, and they were a great source of information. It was not children, but two men who had been in the crowd who approached him. They had been struck by this stranger from the east; it was clear to them that he was not the mountebank he was pretending to be. They invited him to come with them to share a meal, and to discourse of his real purpose. This kind of encounter was not unusual. This was how news travelled, sometimes surprisingly quickly, sometimes appearing to halt at an impassable barrier. The undiscerning accepted stories of cheap magic, and serious news came to those who knew what to look for. The youngest wise man and the two Jews conversed long. To him, it gave the feeling that here he had encountered something of the real faith, something that had given purpose to the Jewish people. The afternoon drew to a close. Finally, they gave him a warning. He might not have realised it, but by now, he and his friends would have aroused the suspicion and jealousy of Herod with all this talk of a new awakening, even the birth of an actual child. It would be well for them not to delay unduly. While so many Roman soldiers were here for the census, little amiss would happen. After that—who knew? It would be well that those to whom Herod might wish ill should be away out of his kingdom.

The young man left. Sad though the picture was overall, he rejoiced at the encounter with two such men. He thanked them, and made for the city gate. As he came to the gate, a hand clutched at his arm. It was the wretch he had saved that morning from the attentions of the crowd. The man spoke in a whisper, cupping his hands round his mouth. It was an ill-educated voice. He looked round, making sure that he could not be overheard. Then he spoke. "Sir, you helped me this morning. I got friends here." He stopped, and looked round again, then went on. "I got a friend works up at the palace—you know where I mean." He jerked his head expressively. "He told me that you and your mates didn't ought to try to see this friend of yours what's having the baby. It won't do her no good, nor the kid, nor you lot either. See? You better get out, quick."

For Balthazar and Melchior Herod's palace had proved neither welcoming nor reverent. Words were fair, but eyes did not smile. They must leave.

The youngest added the account of his day. The beggar's warning had given him this same sense of unease. Next to children, the poor were often the truest witnesses. The high places of the land could dissemble.

For some reason, not clear to any of them, their presence constituted danger—but to whom? They retired to ponder, and to sleep.

The next morning it was clear to all of them that they should depart. Herod's palace had been an unlikely place for their search. Might Bethlehem, "least of all", be the source of some new vision?

11

Unto Us a Son

SOMEWHERE THEN, FROM remote Arabia or Persia, a mission of wise men had been sent out. This hardly seemed to concern Joseph, as he and Mary made their slow steady journey, a journey that would see them, if the Lord granted Joseph's prayer, safely arrived in Bethlehem before Mary's child was born. Like the magi, they too were finding more people on the way than they had anticipated. This was no bad thing. Even the thieves who hang around at the edge of a crowd would be ready to give help. Roman soldiers urged everyone on, and spoke more gently as they caught sight of Mary's heavy figure. "How far are you going, Father?" they called out. An occasional centurion grumbled at the orders that had sent a woman in Mary's condition travelling across the country. But orders were orders, particularly to troops as well disciplined as the Romans. Not much that they could do here. All right, Dad, get along, not too far now to Bethlehem.

Bethlehem came into sight. It had not been too far. What the soldiers had neither said nor known was how crowded Bethlehem would be. It was not for Joseph and Mary to decide that, as Bethlehem was crowded, they would stay outside it or go on elsewhere. Yet in Bethlehem there was no room, no room. Distant relatives had already arrived, and taken up every bed, every space. Wearily, Joseph led the donkey and Mary towards the inn. The innkeeper was some distant relative. But there too, the story was the same. There was no room. Joseph could see for himself. The innkeeper called his wife, "Hannah, Hannah, come." An over-burdened Hannah came hurrying, leaving a mêlée of impatient customers. She took one look at Mary and, like the soldiers, she could have cursed the imperial orders that had brought a poor woman to have a child here in this confusion. She hoped fervently that it was not a first child. Not that there was anything she could do. The best thing, in fact the only thing, was for Joseph and Mary to "go round there", there where the animals were stalled. At least they could take the donkey with them.

It sounded heartless, but to Mary it was comfort enough. There would be shelter and warmth. Joseph would help her, and the time had come.

❄

Some hours had passed before the innkeeper's wife managed to get to the stables. Might her Lord forgive her for the delay; she could not think that He would really understand how much she had needed the money from all those customers.

She was amazed, on reaching the stables, to find a sleeping man-child, a triumphant Joseph, and Mary—Mary with a smile of welcome on her face. "Our thanks to thee, Hannah, for this comfort. See—our baby sleeps." The baby slept peacefully in the noisy stables. "We have called him Jesus."

Hannah and her husband afterwards told different tales of the order in which things had happened. Both agreed that an unexpectedly important part was played by young Nicodemus. He was Hannah's nephew. He came from Jerusalem, from an influential branch of the family. He was the kind of boy who usually found out what was happening. He had, naturally, managed to sneak in and see the baby—"our baby". Then he had gone off up the hill to tell any of his friends who were awake—those boys whose task it was to help the shepherds out watching the sheep. Nicodemus urged them to come. He told them of a wonderful baby, and an angel. There, under the great star. Perhaps it was the star that convinced them. Shepherds and boys, with one left to guard the flock, followed him back to the stable. It was an odd place to come to behold a wonder. They went in cautiously, amid the gentle breathing of animals, the occasional stamp of a hoof. Nicodemus was right. There was the wonder—Joseph, and a little baby sleeping on its mother's breast, and the welcoming smile from Mary, with no thought of "Why are you disturbing us?" Shepherds and boys knelt. One of them asked the baby's name. It was Jesus. The minutes passed. A young shepherd, whose own wife had just had their first child, started to sing a little hymn of praise. Softly, they all joined in: "Hosanna, hosanna."

12

Invitation to the East

FOR JOSEPH AND Mary, it was a time of complete peace. The dreaded journey was over, and the child for which each felt a special responsibility had been born safe and well. Human visitors as well as the animals, thronged. "Our baby" slept unperturbed for hours, was roused for food and slept again, warm in Mary's arms. The innkeeper talked with Joseph, Hannah with Mary. It seemed a happy omen that she had the same name—Hannah—as Mary's own mother. Hannah was continually amazed at Mary's ability to be "at home" in a stable. It was not all that surprising that Mary, young and healthy, should have had such an easy birth, even for a first child, but to be so welcoming all the time, so lacking in any feeling that more ought to have been done for them—*that* was a wonder. The stables took on a new life, as the venue for all kinds of visits. The only shadow of dissent from Mary was when the innkeeper insisted on moving his animals elsewhere, until she realised that it would be as much for their good as for the convenience of visitors. But the shepherds and the boys, and Mary and Joseph, and the innkeeper and Hannah and Nicodemus, would always remember the scene of that first night, when the animals had stood around as if joining in with the human voices singing "Hosanna".

One of the first visitors was the young shepherd, the one who had started the singing. He proudly brought his wife and month-old son. The baby, older than Jesus, would be a bit younger than Elizabeth's John would now be, and Nicodemus said that it was a clever baby. Young Nicodemus, needless to relate, was in and out all the time. Mary had at first thought that this well-favoured lad was the son of the inn, but Hannah had explained. This was her nephew, who lived with his parents in Jerusalem; they were important people, his parents, the father high in the ranks of the Temple. They knew and were known to Zachariah. Young Nicodemus was a boy to enjoy the city ways just as much as the visits to the quieter Bethlehem. Not that *this* visit saw Bethlehem quiet. Hannah added that although the boy was bright, you had to keep your eye on him. Mary thought of the boy John who had accompanied them to the previous Passover, and wondered what questions he would have ready for their return. She laughed over Hannah's story about Nicodemus and his ears. He had come and asked her, one time, to measure his ears; measure his ears? Yes, he had said, because it was being said in Jerusalem that he had longer ears than anyone else in the city. Also, he added, a shorter tongue. Young mischief, said Hannah, though it was true that the child picked up any information going.

It was a period of smiling, unblemished happiness. It seemed as if prophecies of old had been fulfilled. Man lived at peace with man.

Visitors who had come out of idle curiosity ("a boy...born in the stable in the inn...during the census") sat in quiet, awe-struck and wondering. Some were from the little community itself, one or two from further away. The boys who were fortunate enough to have been there "that night" brought along other brothers and sisters. Mothers came with toddlers and babies. Fathers brought along grandparents. A few remembered Joseph's own father, Heli, son of Mattham. Truly a holiday time, and yet a time for quiet reverence. "Our baby" could be looked at (not that you could see much) but his sleep must not be disturbed. The noisiest children stole in like mice from the field.

It would soon be time for Nicodemus to return to the capital, with those travelling that way. Word of the birth had already reached Jerusalem. No one doubted that the stories recounted by Nicodemus would make the event even more dramatic, more vivid. Sad though he was to leave, he had the promise of being able to see "our baby" again soon, as Mary and Joseph returned home. He instructed the other children how to look after the stable—someone always had to stand at the door, to escort in the visitors. After all, it would be a pity not to announce some visiting prince or the archangel Gabriel. You never knew these days.

It was one of Nicodemus's shepherd boys who was "on guard", as he put it to himself, when the most spectacular visit of all occurred. However, the older people would later refer to it, in the minds of the children it was always "the visit of the camels". Great majestic riding camels; each of the three ridden by a king; each king in fine raiment; each bearing in his hand a wrapped and beauteous gift.

With portentous solemn gait, the camels approached. The riders seemed a little bit nonplussed, and the third in the line looked round, as though to ask the way. The boy ran to him. "You are coming to see our baby?" he demanded. There was the slightest possible hesitation, the youngest wise man actually wondering if he should make some jest about the age at which one could have begot "our baby". He decided against it. They had already heard of the wondrous birth that had occurred in the stable, so he simply assented. Yes, they had come to visit the wondrous child.

Balthazar entered first, dismounted, bowed his head before mother and child, and handed his gift to Joseph. Melchior followed. He looked round him with a happy smile, his first smile since leaving, or indeed entering Herod's palace. There, he had felt so strong an impression of evil that he had almost expected to see the scriptural warning of the writing on the wall—"*Mene, mene, tekel, upharsin.*"

But here, here in the stable, was a wealth of loving kindness. He too bowed gravely, and handed his gift to

Mary. The servants drew the camels to one side, to stand with Balthazar and Melchior, behind Joseph, as if painted in by an artist to be the background to Mary and the baby. Last of all, the youngest of the wise men came in. With knee and heel, he guided his camel to where the child lay, and, with a slight touch from his hand, made the camel kneel at Mary's feet. Slowly, slowly he slipped out of the saddle. He held his gift outstretched. For a moment the child awoke, and seemed to gurgle at the coloured wrappings. Mary looked at the camel's head, so close. "He's good," whispered the youngest wise man. "You can touch him."

Mary's hand rested a moment on the animal's forehead. Then she took the gift and looked searchingly at the young man. "How fine it looks," she said, "and you—you are young to be the bearer. May the Lord protect you, ever more."

The three wise men did not withdraw to consult together. There was no need. They were all remembering the words of the beggar: "It won't do 'er no good, nor the kid…better get out, quick." Left here, where Herod's arm could reach, the child might not even grow up, let alone to greatness. It was clear to them that here they had found a family where a child might grow to his proper stature, whether that stature was to be important, or humble and. unknown. All three had the same thought. It was the youngest wise man, standing nearest to Mary, who was to speak for them all. He had always had the gift of eloquence. Might it not desert him now?

"Lady, dear Lady. Dear mother of this baby. We have come across the desert, in search of a great wonder. We have found it—here in your arms. Our prince and our land are truly hospitable, and we ask you that you should come with us. Will you not come? See, this camel, brought up by my own hand, is gentler than any other. You can ride in safety. We have servants, baggage. All shall be for your comfort."

Balthazar moved forward and spoke to Joseph. "It is true. Ours is a land of hospitality, our prince a true worshipper. The Jew is free to worship his own god. Is not Jehovah to be found everywhere in the world? Will he not be there with you? We, through no merit of our own, have wealth at our command. You and your wife and your precious child shall have all that man can provide."

It had not been necessary for the wise men to consult each other before making this offer. It was equally unnecessary for Joseph and Mary to discuss the answer. The strangers were so very kind, extremely kind, and they must not take it amiss that their offer was refused. Joseph and Mary had their own home, in the north, in Galilee, and there they would be going, to be surrounded by their own families. Wealth would not be theirs, but they would be in their own home.

The youngest man looked again at Mary. He made a final appeal. "Lady, the camel shall be yours." He looked round. "And yonder donkey shall come. There are many of us even in our fair land who are motherless. Lady—oh, lady—do come." It was long since anyone had seen tears on the face of the youngest wise man.

The appeal had to go unheeded. Mary and Joseph thanked the men again and again. Hannah and her husband came in and urged them to take refreshment. They stayed the merest time that courtesy demanded and were gone.

The boy "on duty", who had been listening outside the stable, looked a little bit doubtful, as if he thought that the offer of the strangers should have been accepted. Perhaps he was thinking that he might have had a chance of a ride on one of the great camels.

Hannah and her husband joined the family. The refusal to go with the strangers had somehow reminded Mary and Joseph sharply of their own home. They were due to set out in two more days. They again told of what was awaiting them in Galilee. Mary and the baby and Joseph would have Joseph's mother with them (a woman of course who was still remembered by older folk in Bethlehem). It was hoped that she would soon be better. Then in the spring there would be all the excitement of the wedding of Mary's older brother, Reuben; he was marrying Rebecca, from a big family in Capernaum; it was Rebecca's mother who had given them the lovely blue shawl.

The innkeeper enquired about what flocks they had, and was again told about the flocks, and the boisterous ram Jacob, and of course about Mary's brother Benjamin—good-looking, reliable Benjamin who had had to manage so much while Reuben kept going off to see Rebecca. About her father, Mary spoke with gentle pride: a Sabbath was well kept when such a man spoke the prayers. And she thought too of prayers led by Joseph, now the head of his own family. Her thoughts took a leap ahead; she looked down at the baby and thought of the time when he too would be the head of a family, speaking the prayers for them. Hannah asked about Elizabeth's child. As far as one knew, that was a fine child, growing apace. He was called John. This reminded Mary of the other little boy called John, the one who had asked all the questions on the way to Jerusalem. He was like to be another Nicodemus! Mary said she often thought of his question: "Has God stopped speaking to Herod, or had Herod stopped listening?"

The mention of Herod gave a check to the conversation. In any case, it was time for sleep. The next day, the last one in Bethlehem, would be busy preparing for the journey, then one more night at the inn, and then a start on the journey home. Might the Lord bless the innkeeper and his wife, might they be rewarded for all their kindness. As Mary dropped off to sleep, there was a smile on her face, she was dreaming of the hills of Galilee and the voice of her father, as well as of a kneeling camel who sang Hosannah.

The next day was another day of happiness, busy with preparations for the departure. Many came to say goodbye. Some intended to wait till the actual departure in the morning. The wife of the young shepherd brought a special loaf she had baked: "It will keep up your strength on the journey." The innkeeper tried in vain to get Joseph to accept the loan of an ass, larger than the one they had brought with them: it could be sent back when some reliable trader passed that way. Hannah rejoiced at the thought of Mary's return to her own home and the welcome that would be awaiting our baby. The one thing on which no decision was reached was the destination of the gifts from the kings. Clearly, possessions of such value might serve to attract the attention of thieves to the travellers: yet, what could be done with gifts entrusted to them with such a depth of meaning? Would Hannah and the innkeeper accept them? Of course not! The question was unresolved when they retired for the night.

All went early to rest, ready for an early departure. The Lord had given cause for gladness. Might the light of His countenance continue to shine on them.

13

The Flight into Egypt

QUIET UNDER THE STARS, Bethlehem slept. Suddenly, crashing through the stillness of the night, came the sound of two galloping horses. Joseph hurried out, along with the innkeeper. Mary sat up, listening, watching. There was the voice of a boy. It was Nicodemus. It was a frightened Nicodemus; then Joseph's voice, then the innkeeper, incredulous, angry: "You are not telling the truth. You can't be." Again the voice of the boy, protesting and desperate.

Joseph, Hannah and the innkeeper brought the boy into Mary. "It is true," he sobbed, "I tell you it's true." He caught his breath. "Herod has given orders that the guards are to come out and kill all the boy babies in Bethlehem."

Hannah gasped. It could be true. If there was news, Nicodemus would have been the one to hear. For a second they stood transfixed. Nicodemus caught at Mary's hand. "You've got to go, now." He was right. Somehow the boy had heard this dreadful news, and the family must be gone.

In anxiety and confusion, the flight was made ready. There was no question now but that Joseph would take the large ass as well as his own. They must get away, to Egypt. They must take the traders' route. One day, it might be, they could send the ass back, but no matter.

The other babies? Not to think about it, not to think about it. A whole community cannot march away. Even one family, a family not of Bethlehem, cannot be sure of escape. The Lord who has blessed us in the past be thanked that he sent this news from Jerusalem.

Dear God, where is Nicodemus? He was found lying beside the baby. He awoke. He was questioned. How had he come? He explained that he had taken the horse of Flavius, the captain of the guard. Flavius was drinking, they were all drinking, the horse would not be needed till late in the morning. He must get the horse back by dawn. If he did not… . There was no need to complete the sentence; everyone knew the penalty for stealing a Roman horse. Nicodemus must leave at once.

The innkeeper would keep the gifts from the Magi. These at least could be turned into help for stricken Bethlehem. Joseph and Mary must go. Each hour meant an extra hour and so many miles before the Roman soldiers arrived. The donkeys were made ready and the party hurried away, the night dark except for the diminishing light of the great star.

The innkeeper and Hannah stood in the open. They could hear, from the road up to the trade route, the noises made by two laden donkeys. On the road to Jerusalem, the sound had already died away of a boy on a stolen Roman horse, galloping for his life.

Sorrow now engulfed Joseph and Mary. Their feelings of anguish and hopelessness had been obscured in the bustle surrounding their hurried departure. Now, they thought of the horror from which they were fleeing. They thought of the families. Poor doomed families. Proud young fathers, little innocent babies, a mother even now nursing a longed-for first son. Nicodemus, a thief, desperately riding a stolen horse. And why, why had this come to pass? What danger could the powerful Herod think to find in Bethlehem, the least of towns? Great and merciless kings in that eastern world murdered their young relatives, their possible successors, but how could a Bethlehem threaten the kingdom of a Herod?

Behind the fugitives came the sound of hurrying hooves. Joseph heard them first, and was aghast. There were two horses. Surely not Roman soldiers already? As the sound came nearer, it was obvious that these were not fine and well-fed horses. They drew abreast, and a man's voice rang out, oily somehow and ingratiating. It was not a voice to inspire trust. "Ho, mister. It's late to be travelling this road." Joseph agreed. The second man rode up beside Mary, and carefully scrutinised her. "You got your little one along, too." Again Joseph agreed. These were no emissaries of government—more probably thieves escaping justice. The two men appeared to be talking over some scheme. Then the first one spoke again.

"Mister, my friend here and me, we don't like the idea of you and your wife and the baby travelling alone here. 'T'ain't safe, you know. So we are going to ride along with you till the light comes. We'd hate you to fall among thieves, and this ain't a good road. It'll take us a bit longer to ride along with you and the donkeys, but we like to give a hand where we can. Don't we?" he called out to the second man.

For Mary and Joseph, there was no choice. They could not ride away and leave their unwelcome companions, and they dared not stop.

The men, as Joseph had rightly guessed, were malefactors on the run. If intercepted by the law, they had every intention of posing as the brothers or cousins—some relation or other—of the woman with the baby. Not having the information that had reached the long ears of Nicodemus, they were unaware that they were putting themselves into danger by joining a family with a baby leaving Bethlehem that night. As Joseph and Mary did not look like criminals (the men smirked to themselves), they felt they were on to a good thing. "You'll be all right with us, mister," they called out to Joseph.

Morning light brought the ill-assorted little convoy up with a larger group. The men on the horses slipped unobtrusively away. To Joseph, this larger group seemed to offer what he had been hoping for—safe company with honest traders en route for Egypt. He hoped desperately that they would stay long enough for Mary and the donkeys to have a necessary rest.

He was to be disappointed. The caravan had finished their rest. They had lost too much time already. The trader in charge wanted to get home to his wife and children. One of the men looked with pity at Mary and the baby but—what could one do? Can't hang about for every stray on the road. He threw Joseph a bag with a few provisions. "Here, Jew. We can't hang about…too many thieves this way…other traders are due…tomorrow, could be. So long, descendant of Abraham." The caravan moved off. Was this to be the pattern—thieves and rogues for company, honest men too busy to wait? As soon as the contact with other human beings ceased, and the need to make some effort to speak, or answer, horror once more loomed in Mary's mind. She thought of the women of Bethlehem, and looked round her. Ought she to have come away?

Joseph saw the look. He came up to her, and helped her dismount. He pretended a cheerfulness that clearly he did not feel. He asked how the baby Jesus was taking the journey—not a truly necessary question, as the baby had slept quietly most of the way. Now, said Joseph, the night was over and they must eat. He made a great show of spreading out what they had, while watching Mary uneasily. See, here was the welcome bag of provisions that the trader had given them and there was what Hannah had packed, including a special sweetmeat that she had prepared as a present for Rebecca at the coming wedding; and here, finally, so carefully wrapped up was the loaf baked for their sustenance by the shepherd's wife.

Up till now, Mary had not wept. Perhaps the thought of a disaster overcoming the many does not penetrate, as does the news of one single death. That loaf brought before Mary again the picture of the young shepherd, singing Hosanna, and his wife, proudly holding their month-old first-born son. Mary broke down, and wept and wept. She was distraught. She could not be comforted. It seemed to her that they should not be running away. It was wrong. They should be back there, in Bethlehem, sharing with the other mothers. "Joseph," she implored, "Joseph, we must go back."

Joseph too, though not sharing Mary's present doubts, had embarked on this dubious enterprise under the impulsion of Hannah and the innkeeper. Mary's words were doubly a turning point for him. Up till then, he had never felt that he need question her ideas. Now, it was clear to him, as clear as an object lit up by a solitary shaft of sunlight, that Mary was being led only by her own distraught mind. There flashed before him the picture of Mary long ago with the wounded man in the defile. She had not said, "We must go and help." *She* had gone to the man. On the Jerusalem road, she had not called the others to help her...*she* had gone herself to a dying man. If it had now been right for her to go back to Bethlehem, she would have been up and away, with Jesus in her arms, and probably taking the bigger donkey too. That last incongruous thought brought to Joseph a tiny ray of humour in the black situation.

He must show Mary what had been revealed to *him*, Joseph, as the way ahead. He moved closer to her and held her and the baby tightly in his arms. "Mary, my beloved, wife and desire of my heart, here, here in your arms is the baby we must cherish now. In the fullness of time, it will be children of mine that you will hold. Think, beloved Mary, of our children, yet to come." Gently he took the baby from her arms, holding it almost as Abraham might have held Isaac, ready to be sacrificed. "This child has only us. We are his only chance." Mary was quieter. Joseph spoke softly, and ended by adapting the words used by her mother so long ago: "You have courage, Mary, my beloved, a courage that will be unconquerable so long as we are defending something smaller and weaker than ourselves. That is our shield."

Joseph stopped speaking. Mary's tears had ceased. He gave the child back to her and they sat quietly together.

It had been a turning point in two respects. First, there was now no more doubt, no question but that they should press ahead. Also, in some strange way, had been born the pattern that was to last the rest of their married lives. It would not often occur to Mary, a devout and dutiful Jewish wife, to question something proposed by Joseph. On a rare, and sometimes unexpected occasion, she would act on her own, as unquestioningly as when she had broken the Sabbath to help one of her father's animals. It would then not be, "Joseph, Joseph, do let us do this," but an action seen and immediately done. It was not every Jew in that world who would have acknowledged that his wife had insights denied to him. The Lord spoke, but men did not always listen.

They ate. Mary broke off a piece from the loaf made by the shepherd's wife, and handed it to Joseph. As they ate, they thought of the woman who had made the bread; might they, if their lives were spared, ever be ready to help those in need, to remember those who would suffer in Bethlehem, anywhere. Might the breaking of bread in the future remind them of the shepherd's doomed baby, and their resolve. Mary's child had been miraculously saved; perhaps they might sometime repay the debt.

They set out again, slowly making their way towards Egypt. It was so unlike their journey to Bethlehem. Then, although it had been uncomfortably crowded, people had been ready to give what help they could to a woman whose time had come. Soldiers shouting at a crowd had made a path for a pregnant woman on a donkey. Food had been offered. Blessings had been called down on them. Here, on this weary way into Egypt, there might be an occasional act of kindness...but the way was strange, fellow-countrymen few. Up till now, they had lived in their own Jewish world. Authority might produce irrational demands, and thieves and wasters transgress the laws set by the Lord. Your own standing in the community was what you, and, of course, your family, (what was the difference?) had built up over the years. Now, it was clear to Joseph and Mary that they were in a very different world, a world in which malefactors joined you, not as suppliants seeking shelter but as boon companions. Honest traders accorded you less compunction than a man at home gave to his herds.

It was with a new emphasis that Joseph thought of the words of the psalm, "Plead my cause, O Lord, with them that strive against me; fight against them that fight against me, take hold of shield and buckler and stand up for my help."

He led the donkeys forward.

14

Arrival in Egypt

The dangers and discomforts of the journey were only too evident, the disadvantage of being, as so often in their national history, strangers in a strange land. However, just as clouds part and show the sun behind, the fugitives were to realise that there were compensatory advantages. If to some, you will be "Ho, Jew" and "See, descendant of Abraham", to others you will at once be dear as fellow-countrymen in a way that does not happen when all are at home.

An encounter with some Jewish traders heading back for Jerusalem enabled them to despatch the big donkey back to the innkeeper. There was no need to question the honesty of such men. They spent the Sabbath together, and then the Jewish caravan headed for Judea, leaving

Joseph and Mary to push on across the desert. They were beginning to feel safer from pursuit. If Nicodemus had been right, the Roman guard had by now done its work. Joseph and Mary prayed for stricken Bethlehem, and were not sorry to go some hours on their own. "Our baby" gave little sign of having being disturbed by anything. He spent a very short time awake. According to Mary, he was ready to greet anything new with interest and approval. Perhaps she was imagining this. Perhaps she was already seeing the alert happy child that "our baby" might become, if they ever reached the other side of the desert, or it may have been the need to give assurance to the baby that helped Mary to show a hopefulness that she could not otherwise have mustered. This child was to her, and to Joseph, a special responsibility. She must not think of Bethlehem. The child's life must be one of such happiness as they could provide; it would be without reason to have brought him out of danger only to ruin his babyhood with useless lamentation.

Pray God that somehow, some time, they could make a recompense for the sufferings of Bethlehem. When Jesus woke, she sang. She tried to wave his fists to greet birds flying far overhead. She pretended that he understood as she tried to describe to him the incredibly beautiful colours of a sunset seen over the desert.

They started to think of what lay before them in Egypt, of how, above all, would Joseph find work. It was Mary now who showed greater assurance. The fowls of the air had their nests, the foxes their earths: the sons of men would find somewhere to lay their heads.

Another group of south-going traders was encountered.

It enabled Mary and Joseph to go in safety for a few more miles. Then came the Sabbath, and the inevitable parting. The caravan halted only for the night, and was away with the early dawn. The Jews' observance of the Sabbath had seemed odd to the Gentile traders—giving up a safe escort, hope their god provides them with another, eh, by Jupiter? So, long, Jew. They waved to Mary and tried to assure her that all would be well for her and her fine baby. Might her own god protect them.

Their next encounter was the final one. Their adherence to their own ways of worship brought them close. This was a Jewish trading group, one making regular trips to the cities of the Nile, and they would escort them the rest of the way. Jew does not leave Jew stranded. They travelled together.

Again came the Sabbath. In the quiet of that day, there was opportunity for the leader to question Joseph, whom he had already assessed in his own mind as a good man. He was a carpenter by calling? The trader wondered to himself what set of circumstances could have persuaded such a one to take wife and baby and depart on such a journey. And where, by all that was good, were the tools of the man's trade? The trader could see no reason why such people should be travelling; it was the escapade of wasters, running from disaster or discovered crime. Clearly neither Joseph nor the gallant young Mary were such people. In any case, whatever they had done or had done to them in the past, they must think about their future.

Had they perhaps got relatives in Egypt? No, they had not. Well, that might not matter all that much, for in fact there was a small Jewish community existing on the Nile, and that community would take them in. He, the trader, would escort them to within a mile or two of the place. After that, Joseph and Mary would have to take the lower road, which would lead them through those quarters of the town where most of the foreign groups lived—not that the government insisted on it—you could live where you wanted, provided you didn't interfere with all the temples and places sacred to all the different gods. He explained to Joseph where he would have to go and which would be their quickest way to get to the Jewish settlement.

What would Joseph do for money, for getting tools? It would be better to arrive showing, as well as saying, that he wanted work. The trader looked thoughtfully at Mary on the donkey. She had been happy to walk a good deal of the time. He worked out certain sums in his mind. Yes, he had a proposition to make; if Joseph was prepared to part with the donkey, he would pay him such and such a sum, in Egyptian money, and Joseph would have the wherewithal for at least the tools of his trade. Food he need not worry about initially. A stranger in that part of the world would receive food from Jew and Gentile alike, and the first night's lodging. They rejoiced at the trader's thoughtfulness; Joseph had worried about his lack of tools.

He thought, with sudden sadness, of the very different circumstances in which he had first bought the donkey. It seemed a long way from his Uncle Samuel, and Mary's brother Reuben, and that relation of Reuben's espoused, Rebecca, who had procured the donkey for him. And a long time ago that he had gone to fetch Mary from the house of Zachariah. Mary suddenly spoke: "Joseph, dost thee think that Elizabeth's John has teeth yet?"

Whether Elizabeth's John had teeth or not, Jesus and Mary and Joseph would soon be in Egypt, prospecting a new land. The kindness of their fellow-countryman had encouraged them. Too soon they arrived at where their ways separated. A trader on a regular mission had clients, Egyptian clients, that he must visit. The fugitives must take the other road, to where they would find the Jewish and other foreign groups. Might the Lord be to them a guide, as he had been to Moses, a pillar of cloud by day and a pillar of fire by night; might he give them a sure and certain path. His name be praised.

The baby gave a little cough.

Darkness fell suddenly. It seemed that they were approaching habitations, and they halted. An elderly Jewish woman came out and asked what they were doing on the road so late. Joseph explained. At once the woman invited them in...poor strangers, and a baby too; they must stay the night. The house was poor and the food scanty, but for Joseph and Mary it was doubly welcome. It was a roof over their heads for the night, and an opportunity to be once more with their own countrymen.

15

Sojourn in Egypt

THE FAMILY WERE to spend six years in Egypt, a time that would end when Herod died. Without the presence of the baby Jesus, and indeed the obligation they had assumed for him, they might have been tempted to repine, thinking of their homeland, and seeing themselves as exiles, the Nile as their river of Babylon. Whatever their future was to be, they now lived each day with the assurance that for them no time must be wasted, but every experience used for the benefit of Mary's first-born child. It was no different indeed from the feeling that most good parents have, and not only for the first-born; their devotion to Jesus was to them like the ancient pillar of cloud by day and smoke by night to Moses, ever beckoning them on.

The years of exile proved to be not unhappy. Egypt was going through a period of prosperity, the granary of an ever-growing Roman Empire. The lean years foretold by a long-dead Jew were over, and the great grain ships sailed in procession for Rome. Employment could be found for a good workman, particularly if that workman was backed by the solid reputation of the Jewish community. It was not, of course, home, and the casual tolerance of the Egyptian concealed a cynicism that was foreign to the basis of Jewish life. How could there be true worship when each had his own little god, his own brazen image?

Perhaps it was well for Joseph and Mary that the family arrived in Egypt at a time of such abundance. The facade of toleration might have cracked under a wind of adversity, but now there were fair prospects for a hard-working family, which would prove of advantage to Joseph as he set out to look for work.

The morning after their arrival, they went outside to see where they were. Their resting place had not been what they expected. Here was part of no respectable Jewish quarter, such as the trader had told them about. The "house" was on the edge of a straggling collection of hovels and shelters, some already derelict, the kind of place that grows up on the edge of cities, inhabited by the poor and the outcast. The woman came out of the hut and joined them. She explained that she lived here alone with her son; her son was very ill; her son had not very long to live. Would they like to stay with her? There would be room. Joseph hesitated; it was not the kind of place that he had hoped to find. Mary, in what he recognised as being one of her moments of inspiration and decision, said yes, of course, they would stay.

Thus was settled the question of where they would have their home. Mary would now unpack their belongings, and give what help she could to the woman and an ailing man. Joseph must go to the city and find out about work.

He first approached the Jewish quarter, where most of his countrymen lived. It was not difficult to find, and he had a courteous reception. His friend the trader had sent word. The first necessity was for Joseph to acquire tools; the elaborate arrangements made to ensure that he was not cheated over such a purchase naturally took rather more time than the finding of employment. Yes, one man had a brother whose wife's nephew was, in a manner of speaking, a trader in tools, among other things; he would be the person to know where, and at what price, and how soon, the tools could be purchased; Joseph should rely on this man, for it would not be right to let Joseph, as a newcomer, go into the markets. Joseph had the perfectly correct impression that he was being ushered into a city where the newcomer could expect to be fleeced; once established, he would be in a position where he would be expected to take advantage of some new arrival. The cities of the Nile were not famed for over-scrupulousness. After a while, tools were produced for his inspection, and he was watched while making his choice. It was not only the tools that were being judged! His choice was approved—well-worn, but sturdy and sound. Joseph could be recommended. Employment then came without difficulty, as it usually did if the Jewish community spoke up for you. It was not their custom to speak up for rogues and wasters; these, unhappily, existed and must be cared for, but in one's own community; a recommendation to the world of the Gentiles must be honoured.

While Joseph was in the city, the elderly crone who owned the hovel was doing what she could to make Mary feel at home. Her son had little time to live, and she rejoiced that this decent young Jewish couple with the nice baby were prepared to stay. The scene was set for the sojourn in Egypt.

It was a period in which new names were to come into the family's history. Instead of Reuben and Benjamin and Rebecca there would be Vashti, and James, and Rachel. James did not come for another two years, Rachel for four. There would be four new names if you counted Gracious Princess Taroth, and she was not even born till later.

Vashti's arrival was heralded by a loud and penetrating wail, the very first morning, from outside the door. Mary hurried out. Outside the next hut, in the morning sunlight, sat the kind of young slattern one would have expected. The youngest wise man would have greeted her as a Queen of Sheba. The slattern gave a carefree wave of her hand to Mary. "Greetings, stranger. Greetings and welcome. Art thou to be a neighbour?" She might have been deaf, so little did she pay attention to the child bawling beside her. That, explained the elderly crone, that child is Vashti. As Mary seemed to be showing some anxiety about Vashti, the Queen of Sheba explained that this was her daughter. "Three years old, and the plague of all our lives. Vashti," she shouted, "Vashti, stop that bellowing. May Anubis bite you." She added laconically that the child probably wanted something to eat.

Poor child, thought Mary, and provided not only bread, but distraction. She talked to Vashti. She took her in to see the baby. "Look, Vashti, this is our baby. His name is Jesus. See, he has woken up, and he is going to look at you." Mary was thinking that it would have been odd if he had *not* woken up in all that uproar. She also supposed that everyone within earshot would be hastening to see what ailed Vashti, but she was wrong. The shouts and screams were so frequent that neighbours paid no more attention than they did to the cry of the gulls in the harbour. That Vashti. They had even given the word a new meaning, and "Vashti" was the word commonly used to indicate an uproar. What a Vashti there was in the city today, one would say to another.

Vashti, when washed, turned out to be a pretty child. She was well aware of her own attractions, and traded on this to go unscathed into many a place of ill-repute. But now that there was a *baby* to look after, as well as its mother to give you food, she was ready to stop home and play the part of nursemaid. In many ways, she was an exemplary little helper, sitting long hours beside Mary. Vashti's mother soon began to address Mary as "Mary, Holy Mother". Mary was both embarrassed and amused by this. Vashti shortened the name to "Ro–li–ma", and the neighbourhood soon resounded to cries of "Rolima, Rolima", as Vashti spent more and more time in the company of Jesus, or, as she herself put it, "looking after our baby". After a while Vashti grew bored with sitting still. Would kind Rolima let her take Jesus as far as that tree? She would take ever such good care of him. As the months passed and became years, the habit grew, and "as far as that tree" became very much further. Long, long afterwards, when the family were safely back in Galilee (and Mary was no longer Mary, Holy Mother to an idle neighbour) Mary came to realise how much Vashti had contributed to the upbringing of Jesus. He had gone with her into the company of all sorts of men, and. women, most of whom would never have crossed the threshold of his parents' home. Thus the very word "Gentile" was never a reproach in the mind of the little boy; it was a description of people who were not of his own religion; it no more implied contempt than it was to say that so-and-so was a mason, while your own father was a carpenter, though of course, carpenters were best. Vashti was a Gentile. So were—the little boy could pretty soon have mentioned a number of names of the very odd set of delightful acquaintances that, unbeknown to Joseph and Mary, he was making in the time they were in Egypt.

Joseph worked long hours away from home. The son of the house grew worse, and died. Vashti had been the first newcomer to join in with the family. The second was James, Joseph's own son, born to Mary in the little hovel when Jesus was two years old. There were no shepherds and no boys and no animals, but the parents, and Jesus, and the elderly Jewess and the prostitute from next door and her daughter, all joined in singing a very happy "Hosanna".

This was one of the moments when they would most have rejoiced at news from "home". They had sent word of their safe arrival. Had it reached Nazareth? One or two traders had brought word to them; it seemed that their families were well. There had been word of a wedding in Capernaum—Rebecca's and Reuben's? Later on, a rug-seller passed, and it seemed to Mary that it must be her father of whom the man spoke. But why was the man so certain that there was only one son living with his father? Had Reuben...? Or...Benjamin? If the Jewish community on the Nile had been ones to go to the Passover, news would have been more definite. Someone, they said, would be going next year, but they had been saying that for a long time.

James was as good a baby as Jesus had been. He did not have the same experiences as Jesus had endured in his early months, and no camels blew on his sleeping face. For Joseph and Mary, this was another *special* child, special in an entirely different way; the first child of Joseph and Mary. Vashti, now five years old, was jealous of a rival in the affections of Jesus; for a while, the neighbourhood again resounded with "the Vashti" of an uproar. Jesus was his usual sunny self, and allowed himself to be taken off by Vashti on more distant expeditions than Rolima would have chosen. But, she thought, one had to try to do something for Vashti. The poor child was not likely to have much to look forward to in her future as an Egyptian prostitute.

Mary found herself fully occupied now, with three little ones to care for—the baby James, Jesus, and next door's Vashti. The old lady too had been ill; perhaps she had reached a stage of life when she needed help rather than giving it. Mary was glad that Jesus and Vashti could be away out in the sunshine while she tended the baby and sat with the old lady.

It was Joseph who made the astounding discovery, while about on his daily work, that Jesus had learnt to swim. Learnt to swim. The fishermen of their own home, Galilee, were fishers and boatmen, but not...not swimmers and divers. But the child out there in the river, and far from the shore, was undoubtedly Jesus. Joseph was amazed. Probably it had all started months ago with Vashti playing on the riverbank and letting Jesus fall in.

Mercifully the Lord had protected Jesus, and now he could swim, a very alien ability. Joseph told Mary, and it was another thing that they treasured in their hearts. Joseph thought of stopping the expeditions to the water, and was withheld by Mary. Might not the Lord be speaking in unexpected ways to Jesus, as He did to her? They must be very careful over *James's* upbringing. The Lord had already preserved Mary's child Jesus through perils untold: in His power must they trust, while being rather more careful with James.

James had reached the age of two years, quite safely, when the next of the family came. This was a daughter, named Rachel. As the first *daughter*, she too had a special place. James added his infantile voice to the Hosanna.

The family prospered. It was a time they would remember as happy. They could have moved to a better house, but it would not have seemed right. Joseph was never without work. Mary herself was ever busy, with her own three children of six and under, and the nine-year old Vashti, and the old woman, as well as the many small children who turned up and demanded help from

"Ro-li-ma", who washed and bandaged, and dispensed encouragement and good advice. Rachel was now nearly two years old. It was only Jesus who could swim.

The family sat thoughtfully together one Sabbath, Joseph intoning the prayers. There was great thankfulness in his heart that he, a foreigner, had had work, and that they were living in a household where they could all join in worship. He also thought of their own families back in distant Galilee, and the great Jewish celebrations, and above all of the Passover. He prayed for the well-being of whoever in their families lived. He wondered when, if ever, it would be "next year in Jerusalem" for them. Even when Herod died, rumour already reporting that he was a sick man, how would they ever have the wherewithal to pay for the journey back? The nightmare journey of their arrival was not to be repeated. As he prayed, his head bowed, the voice of Vashti broke in. She knew all about their funny old praying, and she would usually hesitate to interrupt, but now she called out urgently, "Ro-li-ma, Ro-li-ma, come here please."

This could not be sheep or bullocks in distress, but Mary went out. There were Vashti, and a small boy who held up a bedraggled white kitten. "Rolima, he's hurted." Mary took the animal and felt it over. The little creature was thin, and dirty, but not badly hurt. Also it was a she and not a he. Mary gently pushed the children aside; the kitten should have something to drink, and then they would put it in the corner there, and let it have a nice sleep. Later that evening, they were saying in the city that one of the sacred white kittens was missing from its place in the Temple.

The attendant who came searching the next morning was surprised that they should have looked after the animal. Keeping a sacred cat, and one that was not well, was a risk that drew down on you the wrath of the gods and the authorities. Most people would have dodged out of any such position. But Gracious Princess Taroth (this was who the kitten was) seemed well. "If thy husband comes to the Temple, he shall be rewarded." It wouldn't hurt them, being foreigners, he thought, if he let it be known that they were under the special protection of Gracious Princess Taroth.

It was another link in the family's comfortable sojourn in Egypt. Mary was sad to notice the splendour of the basket in which the white kitten was taken away. Deifying animals was to her another example of that hollowness that she found at times in Egypt. There was so much that was good and splendid, so many of the people so friendly and utterly uncensorious. Although there were the hills to wander over, there were the wide, wide skies that arch over a country as flat as Egypt. There were the stars, the myriad shining stars and the huge clusters. There were sunsets of a desert splendour. All these spoke to Mary of the power and might of Jehovah, who had in his great mercy proved to be a redeemer to her and Joseph and the children. How pretty the little kitten had looked, curled up in the corner, and how dreadful that some people should think of it as a divinity that ruled their lives, instead of a manifestation of a divine power that had created all things.

16

Return

HERODWAS DEAD. The news, important enough to be transmitted through the Roman legions, speedily reached Egypt. Herod was dead! This meant that Joseph and his family could return; return at last to their own home, exiles no longer.

This immediate hope was followed by the appreciation of the immediate need. They could only return to their own home if Joseph could muster enough money for proper arrangements to be made. There was not going to be any repetition of that unprepared dash, across the desert, merciful though the Lord had been to them then. Soberly, Joseph and Mary realised that any journey away from Egypt must depend on getting more money.

As if their prayers were being answered, one thing after

another speeded their preparations. First of all, there was the totally unexpected beneficence of the grateful guardians of Gracious Princess Taroth. Joseph went up to the Temple, as requested. The loss of the white kitten had happened at some particularly unfortunate moment for its guardians; some event, far from the ken of Mary and Joseph, had made authority especially sensitive about missing deities, and when Joseph appeared he received a reward far beyond his expectations. What an amount! Why it even made the journey possible, no longer some impossible dream. All could be made ready.

Joseph then went and informed his employer that he was leaving. Even from him, there was a small leaving present "to see you safe away from Egypt".

The Jewish community came to give yet further help. They were making arrangements for the old woman, who could no longer live alone; she was being brought into the Jewish quarter, where she would live with her elderly cousins Miriam and Gideon. Also, they were providing Joseph with a certain sum of money for the journey. This was not something that always happened, but the lives of Joseph and Mary had enhanced the reputation of the Jews. Joseph had proved a very good workman, faithfully fulfilling his contract with an employer who still seemed to feel that bricks could be made without straw, work achieved without the provision of proper material. Yes, Joseph had enhanced the reputation of the Jewish community. And Mary too, living in that wretched hovel without complaining, and looking after the old woman as well as her own children. Good children, especially James and the little girl. Jesus, too, was quite a good child, though...it was the first time that the elders of the community were to whisper about the life Jesus led and the wild company he got into. You could hardly blame his father, who was working the long hours of the Egyptian working-man, and of course the mother had the other two little ones; it wasn't so much that they thought it was wrong for Jesus to go round with children like the prostitute's daughter—children after all don't understand—but was it really quite right for him to *enjoy* such company? The elders shook their heads a little, before agreeing that Jesus was only a little child, that it was not the parents' fault and that the family should be given some help for the journey.

Adequate arrangements were being made for the journey. Two suitable donkeys were obtained, this time by Joseph. It was agreed that the journey would be done in the company of a well-known Jewish trader; where they would meet up with him, the position of the stopping-places, and the length of the journey—all was planned and known ahead of time. James, four years old, went round reciting in order the names of the places where they were going to stop. Jesus named the donkeys Balaam's Ass and Daddy's Donkey, and, then went to question his mother about the incident of the angel and Balaam. According to Daddy, the angel had told Balaam to stop, and then the ass had stopped, which was of course the right thing to do, but what about *afterwards*? Had the angel explained to Balaam's ass that it must start being obedient to Balaam again? Some of her son's questions always reminded Mary of the boy John on the way to Jerusalem. How did you know when God was speaking to you? Her answers appeared to satisfy Jesus, who then ran off to find Daddy and ask him what Balaam's ass had been called.

Joseph was in great demand. After satisfying Jesus, he suddenly found a disconsolate Mary. She was not sure about the arrangement that the Jews were making for the old lady to go into the city to live with an elderly cousin, Miriam, and her husband Gideon. Would the old lady be all right? "Joseph, Joseph, oughtn't we to take her with us? She has not so many years to live… . Joseph, surely she could come with us? Joseph, she can go on one of the donkeys, and I can walk." Joseph recognised this as no voice of God. If Mary had been sure, she would already have told the old woman and packed her things. He thought carefully; it wasn't only that it would be difficult to take her, but more that her rightful place was here, in Egypt. He drew Mary to him. "Mary, my love, our nation here is Jewish, but not as we are. For people here, this is home. They are not, as we have been all this while, refugees and exiles. Why think you that no one goes up to the Passover? Many could afford to go. But this for them is home. It would be no kindness to take our old friend away from the sun of Egypt, only to become an exile with us." It was true. Indeed, to Mary's surprise, the old woman was pleased about going to live in the city in the crowded Jewish quarter.

Vashti was spending more time away from the family. The nine-year-old had benefited from Mary's influence and the company of Jesus. She was deeply sorry that they were going, so that even her mother was taking the trouble to find occasions when Vashti, but not Jesus, had to go to friends in the city. Pity Mary and her family were going, thought Vashti's mother, they had been nice neighbours—might the river gods or sacred Isis or someone turn up something for her. She had an idea though...yes...she had an idea.

Gradually everything was worked out, the packing done, the bundles prepared, donkeys made ready. The time had come for the final leave-taking. Much of Mary's time in Egypt had been spent in or just outside their home. She had cared for her own children, for Vashti, for the old woman, and before that for the old woman's dying son, all without very much opportunity to move far from her own home. "Ro-li-ma" had not had much time to wander. It was therefore all the more surprising when so many people came to pay a final visit; some of them were the well-established leaders of the Jewish fraternity, colleagues with Joseph in maintaining that outpost of Jewish faith and life.

For Joseph, the greatest surprise was the number and enormous variety of those who came along "to say goodbye to the kid". Joseph had not expected to receive parting gifts from three of the town's best-known prostitutes, nor indeed their attendance in person. He had long known, and tried to avoid, the ruffianly trader "Black Mohammad", who now appeared, thrusting money into Mary's hands ("My own child is of the age of your son Jesus and is blind. Vashti and Jesus have often come and played with him.") Joseph thought of the contrast between their hunted and poverty-stricken arrival, and this outpouring of gifts and love and affection. How much, he thought, how much was due to the spirit of his wife.

He thought again of the special position that he shared with her for the future of the merry-hearted Jesus. Might the Lord continue to protect them all, might their prayers ever rise.

Finally the family moved away. The last thing that they heard was the outburst from Vashti. She had been enjoying the presence of so many of her acquaintances, especially her "aunties", and had made a point of bringing them to see little Rachel. All of a sudden she had become aware that Mary was leaving, and taking Rachel, and James was going, and so was Jesus. The air was rent with the outraged howls of earlier years. She shouted that Jesus was not to go: "He's got to stay, he's got to stay, and I'm going to marry him." Restraining hands held the little girl, but as the party moved steadily away, they could hear her final yells. "You can't marry anybody else. You've got to marry me. You can't marry anybody else…not anybody else."

Mary was surprised that Jesus was so unperturbed. He was one to want to help anybody in distress. Presently he pulled Mary's head down and himself stretched up to whisper to her. "Ro-li-ma, that was a Vashti, Vashti of a noise, wasn't it?" He smiled reflectively, as one who had a pleasant memory of something, and wishes to share it. "Vashti doesn't really mind that we are going. Do you know what they are doing now? They made me promise not to tell you before we left. Vashti and her mother are going to move into our house, because they say it is better than theirs. And they are going to have a wonderful party tomorrow. They wanted me to come too. But of course…" At this point Jesus went into gales of mirth. "If we had still been there, they wouldn't have been having a party." Mary smiled too. Perhaps she had misjudged Jesus.

Joseph, seeing the other two so much amused, remarked to James that *they* must be serious, and pulled such a long face that James too burst out laughing. It was a happy group on its way to join the caravan. Only Rachel missed the joke, as she was asleep.

17

Home Again

PLEASANT AND REWARDING had been the years in Egypt. The family had arrived there penniless, wanderers, outcast from their homes, the haunting threat of death over the baby, and their marriage in front of them to build. They returned as a happy and united family, encouraged by the community they were leaving, sure of a loving welcome in the place to which at last they were returning. The journey home had been well planned, and everything went smoothly. Mary and Joseph had to make each day enjoyable for the children, hiding, not very successfully, their own growing impatience. At last they parted from their travelling companions outside Jerusalem, with mutual thanks for their time together and hope to meet again at the Passover. Then came the final stages, each mile bringing recognition of some landmark, and the nearer they drew to Galilee, rumours and items of news from others met on the roads. And then—at last—Nazareth was in sight. Nazareth—home—people—people assembling in a great crowd to welcome then, the tall figure of Benjamin overshadowing everyone else—Benjamin, and then Joseph's uncle, Uncle David. Children in Nazareth, like Nicodemus, had long ears, and the news was no sooner known than it had spread. Mary and Joseph are home again. Mary and Joseph have three children. Mary and Joseph have five children—this was not correct, though to Mary it seemed that she had a score or more there were so many flocking round. Everyone possible, in an incredibly short time, assembled to greet them.

The salutations and greetings were followed by the clamour of questions. It was "Where is...?" and "How is...?" from Mary and Joseph, and "How old?" and "What is his name?" and "What have you called her?" from those welcoming them. Gradually they began to take stock. Joseph's mother was alive, not strong now, but fairly well, and living in her brother's house. Mary's own Uncle David had died. Mary's father, who had been summoned, came hurrying down the hill, looking the same tower of strength that he had always been to her. And the quiet young woman with the baby who came down soon after—they were Benjamin's wife and their first-born. Reuben? Where is Reuben? Reuben and Rebecca? No need to worry, no need at all. Mary remembered the wound on Reuben's leg? It had never healed completely; it had become obvious that Reuben ought not to attempt the tough existence of the hills, and he had taken up a shopkeeper's post in Capernaum, obtained through one of the many branches of Rebecca's family. So that itinerant rug-seller had been right thought Mary, when he told them back in Egypt that only one son remained on the farm. Reuben would be over soon to greet the returning wanderers. Yes, and Rebecca had three children, all boys, now aged five and three and one, just between Mary's children. Mary, they joked, must keep a tight hold on the little Rachel, for Rebecca dearly wanted a daughter, particularly such a pretty little girl as Rachel. Rachel, who had alternately slept and wept for the journey, was now quite ready to smile on one and all. And where was Jesus? Where had the boys disappeared to? Mary caught sight of Jesus, and could have wept with joy as she saw him standing there with his grandfather, hand already clutched in hand, the two apparently ready to set off together on some great journey. Now where was James? Ah, there. James was carefully holding one of the donkeys (Balaam's ass); in one of his rare playful moments, he was being the angel, stopping the ass from moving; it was fortunate that Mary was at hand, or no one would have known.

The questions presently gave way to invitations. It was not just one old woman in a hovel now who was ready to welcome them in. But Joseph and his Uncle Samuel had speedily made arrangements. It would be to his uncle's house that they first went, where business arrangements too could be discussed. The next day would be the day for the visit to the farm on the hill. Jesus was ready to go immediately to the hills, so he could go at once, with his grandfather; Jesus departed, assuring his parents that he was going to help his aunt to carry the little baby. He added that she looked just like Rachel.

The threads of their lives were ready to be picked up again. Of the first importance was finding work, and it was quickly settled that Joseph should again be a carpenter, working in his uncle's workshop, with the status of a partner. To herself, Mary uttered a prayer of thankfulness that he would no longer need to be away from home all the daylight hours. Uncle David was glad of someone to share his responsibility: "The Lord has preserved my strength most wonderfully, but I am getting old. The time will come when I can no longer work, and I must prepare for that time. Your mother too can do with more of your company, Joseph, for she is very frail. You and your family will live here too, for there is room enough in the house (we are not the family we once were). There is room here for a growing family—with which we pray the Lord will bless you." Thus simply it was settled.

It was hardly surprising to Joseph to see his mother so much enfeebled; he had hardly dared to hope to see her alive. What was surprising was *her* comment, confirmed by Uncle David, that Joseph looked so much older. The years under an Egyptian sun had taken more toll than he or Mary had realised.

The first visit to Mary's old home set the pattern for the next few years. James, relieved of his task as Balaam's ass's angel, found great contentment in the company of Uncle Benjamin and Uncle Benjamin's quiet wife. James enjoyed being up on the farm helping; he quite liked being about with the animals, and what he liked most of all was *counting* them; wasn't it good when Uncle had brought them all in for something, and you knew that every one of them was in the right place? Actually, this was what Uncle Benjamin liked too, and James and Uncle Benjamin had much in common.

Jesus, who had spent so much of his six and a half years in the back streets of an Egyptian city, was ready to shout with joy as he made his way round to "Grandfather's". When Mary came up on the first morning after their arrival, Jesus was almost incoherent as he tugged her hand to come and see...this...and this over here. "Look, Mummy, Grandpa said this was the stone where you got up to ride the Roman horse. You never told us you rode a Roman horse, Mummy. What was he called? Was he a brown one? And did *you* really tell him where to go, or was he listening to an angel? Or were you? And, look, Mummy, come over here and see where you used to get the water from, and where we are putting in some new steps." Mary noted with interest that it was "we" who were putting in the new steps. It reminded her of her own childhood, and of the discoveries that had opened up as she went further and further afield. After a while, she left Jesus to go on exploring, while she went and sat with her father, and they started to talk over all that had happened. For a long time that first day, they sat quietly together, in great thankfulness for the blessings they had received.

It took many visits for Mary and her father to have time to fill in the great gaps in their lives. That Mary was in good health and spirits was obvious. She had fared well. That was the chief thing, thought her father, though he did not say that Joseph had aged a good deal, a good deal. Mary, asking her father about the past years, finally heard from him of his periods of despair when she had not returned from Bethlehem and their messages had not reached him. The opening words of the Psalm had so often come to him: "My God, my God, why hast thou forsaken me?" He acknowledged that for a while he had been tempted to recite only the opening verses. What he was feeling was indeed expressed in, "O my God, I cry in the daytime, but thou hearest not..." And then, he said, gradually he had been carried on towards the end of the Psalm and had felt that the Lord was still his protector. The end verses were full of triumph. "All the ends of the earth shall remember and turn unto the Lord: and all the kindreds of the nations shall worship before thee." The later verses, said Mary's father, were so much more comforting than the earlier ones. He had learnt to accept, and now he was being rewarded one hundredfold for his steadfastness. To think, he might have despaired, and fallen sick, and never seen Mary again or the three fine children that she and Joseph had brought back from Egypt. On this occasion he finished by asking where Jesus had gone.

While Mary and her father talked, the young Jesus would go further and further afield. It would not be long before, as in Egypt, he was venturing much further than any of the "grown-ups" realised. Mary's talks with her father were often ended with the reminder from James: "Aunt has our dinner ready. Jesus is not back."

Much of the pattern of their daily lives had been settled. They had work, they had their home, they were fulfilling their obligations to parents. There was one more thing for the home-coming to be completed—going up to Jerusalem for the Passover. Not till then would they feel they had at last really come home.

They had returned in the autumn of the year. The following spring, when Jesus was seven, they set out, along with Mary's father, with Benjamin and his family, and many friends and neighbours, on the long-awaited "pilgrimage" to Jerusalem. The boy John who had asked all the questions had gone elsewhere with his parents. Mary realised that the presence of her own children meant that she would not again be as carefree as on that other journey when her father had been "the boy singer". Even with the children though, it was not a hard task when there was someone like Joseph there to help. The Lord had indeed caused his face to shine upon them. It was another happy journey.

If the Passover was the greatest religious occasion of the year, it was also the great meeting place for the scattered members of the Jewish families; those whose marriages had taken them to faraway places, those who were only distantly related. For Mary, this Passover meant the renewal of the ties between her and Elizabeth, and also the start of the bond between her own son Jesus and Elizabeth's son John. The women embraced, and plied each other with questions. Zachariah yet lived, but be was old and frail. He no longer took part in services or conducted prayers. He was not able to get to Jerusalem this year for the Passover; Elizabeth was apologetic about being there without him, but, she explained, they both felt that it was so important that their son should not miss a Passover. Another member of the family (there was always some other member of a Jewish family—even the old woman in the Egyptian hovel had a distant cousin) was looking after Zachariah. And how had Mary fared, and her kind husband Joseph (thinner than Elizabeth remembered him when he had come with the donkey to fetch Mary home)?

Mary recounted with joy that she and Joseph had a growing family. That was well, said Elizabeth; her John of course was, and would always be, an *only* child. Mary told some of the many things that had happened to them, and what had been sad or difficult was quite forgotten as she told of the homecoming, and how well her father was, and how each child was growing up in some *special* way. Her oldest, Jesus, was an adventurous one, and ever eager to be out to see something fresh. John, said Elizabeth, was another such. Although not eight years old yet, he had learnt so much already about the services and the readings, where one and another should stand, and about the Law and the Prophets. She added that John had even told her where one of the priests had made a mistake, and Mary was never sure whether Elizabeth was proud of this, or apprehensive of what it might lead to. Jesus, she thought to herself, was so kind and interested always, that he would not be likely to criticise; a child who had enjoyed the company of Black Mohammad and Queens of Sheba was hardly likely to find the conduct of the priests of the Temple amiss.

In this, Mary was to be proved wrong. The two boys met. John, only six months older than Jesus, was appreciably taller. He had probably had more to eat in the first years of his life. He was a serious-minded little child, and one would almost have thought that he saw his destiny as taking the place so long and so honourably held by his father. Jesus was delighted to be in his company, and the two boys explored the city, John leading and explaining, Jesus as happy going with him to long Temple ceremonies as he had once been in visiting the more dubious quarters of a Gentile city on the banks of the Nile.

By the middle of the Passover, Jesus was full of a new set of questions for his mother. Had Ro-li-ma noticed the man (a scribe, was he?) who was praying at the street corner? Why did he have to wait to start praying until he was sure people were watching him? Why hadn't he clapped his hands together, or borrowed a bell from the lepers, if he had wanted to be sure of an audience? Jesus showed Ro-li-ma some of the tricks he still remembered from Egypt—that was how you attracted an audience. Mary suspected that Jesus perfectly well knew the answers to his questions, so she asked him if he had seen some of the poor people who were giving money—oh yes, he had seen some, especially that poor woman, quite ragged, who had put the two very tiniest coins there in the bowl. Were there many people as poor as that? When be grew up, he thought he would rather be a poor good man than like that other—and he used a somewhat impolite Egyptian word, which Mary did not know that he knew.

It was not only John and Elizabeth whom they met at the Passover. Carefully seeking them out, came a fine looking young man, whom Mary and Joseph at first failed to recognise. It was Nicodemus, who looked with great interest at Jesus, and then asked him what he thought about Jerusalem, and waited for the boy's answer. Jesus said that it was wonderful, except for that funny man praying so noisily at the corner of the street. Then Nicodemus told him all sorts of interesting things and made little jokes; Jesus must not worry about some of the things he saw, some men were only showing off, but there *were* great teachers and rabbis, and when Jesus was bigger, he would meet them—come, are we not all poor wretches sometimes and cheer ourselves up with fine tales and acting as if we were someone big? He held out his arms to show someone being big, and Jesus burst out laughing. Mary was grateful for this interpretation.

When Jesus moved off again (probably in search of John), the others had the opportunity to talk further. There were many questions to ask about Bethlehem. They had heard that Hannah and the innkeeper were well. Yes, indeed. No need to ask if Nicodemus had got back all right that fearful night. They all fell silent, Nicodemus wondering how much had already reached the ears of Joseph and Mary. He decided to give a brief outline only. It had been the most dreadful night, the Roman guards finally came, two days after Joseph and Mary had left; the soldiers had been made drunk before they came. Nicodemus hurried on to more cheering news; what good use Hannah and her husband had made of the presents entrusted to them. Nicodemus picked out "success" stories, how such a one now had three children, and the son of one was so good, and of another so clever; and some of the older children whom they would remember were doing so well… . He was glad that they did not ask about the young shepherd. Finally, they parted, with the promise to see each other again next year.

Mary and Joseph and their family returned to their home in Nazareth, conscious of really being *home* again now that they had been up to the Passover. Mary thought about Elizabeth and her son John and was again thankful for the presence of Joseph.

15

No Longer a Child

THE NEXT VISIT to the Passover was eagerly awaited but did not come till Jesus was twelve. The first year there was a young baby, "special" as their first daughter to be born in Galilee. The next year saw the final illness and the death of Joseph's mother, who passed gently away, murmuring to herself the names of the children. The following year Mary was again with child, and Joseph would not risk the journeyings that had accompanied Mary's first pregnancy. Finally, Joseph was unwell one year, and, unwillingly indeed, allowed it to stop another visit.

It was at this time, when Joseph was ill, and when Jesus was eleven, that Mary decided the time had come to tell Jesus the full story of his birth. She and Joseph had long talked together about what to tell Jesus about his parentage. That Joseph was not his father in one sense, Jesus already knew before leaving Egypt. It would have been wrong to let him come back to Galilee and to risk the information being blurted out in some critical, or worse, irreverent and flippant, way. Joseph had been certain of that. It was Mary who would judge when more was within the child's understanding. That time had come.

Mary spent some time away from her family, wandering again in the hills. She was not concerned with making an excuse for herself, but wanted to be certain that Jesus, even though a child still, understood the love he had received from Joseph. She talked long with her father, and they sought guidance. The temptation might be simply to give a dramatic description of the scene of finding the dying man in that shelter outside Jerusalem, though, as her father pointed out, it was *Jesus* now and not Mary who had become the one in the family to tell an arresting tale. The actual details, including the quite uncertain identity of the dying man, were not important. What mattered, said her father gravely, was to tell of *three* things—her willingness to try to interpret the will of God—the man's desire to stay alive until a child was begotten—and then the infinite care and tenderness of Joseph. This seemed right to Mary, and it was in her father's company, at the finish, that Mary told Jesus the whole story. As might have been expected, Jesus accepted the story with great seriousness. He sat silent. After a while, he made the comment that as his mother had been obeying the voice of God, it made him, Jesus, very much the son of God. He repeated this several times. Then a smile came over his face as he reminded them that as well as God for a father, he had Daddy as well, just like James and the others. Mary always thought from then on Jesus began to show a sense of looking after people as well as just enjoying their company.

The following year, when Joseph was quite recovered, and Jesus was twelve, the next visit to the Passover took place. A great gathering of family and friends went up together, and the journey was enlivened by the games of the children. The younger boys had picked up some funny pieces of wood, which they said were "crowns". Each evening they took turns in being Saul and David and Solomon. Presently they started to argue about which was the greatest, producing some interpretations of the scriptures that would have startled their elders. When the argument became fierce, Jesus produced another "crown", which he said should be for the one who was "the King of the Jews". The younger boys were quite prepared to accept this, only Jesus must come and play and be the King of the Jews: things always went well when Jesus played too. So Jesus was the King of the Jews that evening. On the next evening Mary was surprised to see that it was a girl, her eight-year old daughter Rachel, who was wearing the crown. Jesus explained, "Ro-li-ma, Rachel wanted to play, so she had to be a queen, and the one we thought of was Jezebel. And Rachel cried when she thought we were going to throw her to the dogs, but really it was only pretend—we were going to put her down where the sheep could come and smell her. So I gave her *my* crown instead." So that was why *Rachel* was parading round as "the King of the Jews". Jesus added that he didn't think he would want to be King of the Jews unless he could have Gentiles there too, as Jews on their own were a bit long-faced sometimes.

It was not so often that Mary was called "Ro-li-ma" now, usually when Jesus had some joke to share with her. It took her back to Egypt, and she thought of their time there and further back still to the visit of the wise men. Had they not given them more than those lavish and expensive gifts? Joseph had acquired some of the quiet assurance of the first one, Balthazar. And surely Jesus had some of the merriness and kindness of the youngest? Everywhere he was loved, as those usually are who are ready to love and not to censor. In Egypt, so long ago, he had liked people who would have been accounted sinners. She did not, of course, liken herself to Melchior, though anyone who had known them both would have recognised the same inner vision, the same disregard of external trappings. She wondered if the older magi were still alive, and if, somewhere away in the east, the youngest was leading a people to live at peace with the creation around them.

It was another happy journey, followed by celebrations in Jerusalem, which were of the most solemn. The Passover was always a great occasion, and from time to time came one that stood out in the memory, as on that particular occasion. As Nicodemus had foretold, great leaders and teachers were emerging. Nicodemus, knowledgeable as ever, had encountered, or rather sought out, Jesus and Elizabeth's John, and steered them to those teachers most likely to be have the right words of inspiration and learning. Zachariah had died since their last visit. He had taught John well, and John, taller and that little bit older than Jesus, knew his scriptures. Jesus had learnt well too, from his grandfather and from Mary, but was more anxious that the scriptures should be taken seriously, now, today, by everyone around. The questions from the two boys and their rapt attention made it a time memorable to their teachers. What might they not become? Was it in this generation that the prophecy of Isaiah would be fulfilled with the coming of the Messiah? There were priests and teachers who would have been less welcoming to "young upstarts", and some who would have feared a path leading to—who knows—a holy war to drive out Rome? At the end of the Passover, John had to leave with his mother, but for Jesus and his teachers there was still much to enquire into. The questioning and the expositions went on, the teachers amazed at what they were experiencing and afraid, almost, to interrupt. They felt that you did not interrupt when God was speaking to you even if it was through some unlikely voice. These two boys—what promise for the future, from either, or even from the two together?

Joseph and Mary started the journey back unperturbed at the apparent absence of Jesus. They were well accustomed to his independence, and there were plenty of other relatives he could have been with. He might well have wanted to spend more time with John, and therefore have gone a little way with John and Elizabeth; perhaps even now he was hurrying to rejoin his own party. Jesus, however, did not appear, and Mary was seized with anxiety. "Joseph, Joseph, we must go back; James will help his Uncle Benjamin to look after the others: Jesus is not here, and we must go back. Joseph, Joseph, surely we should go, now, without wasting any more time." It did not seem to Joseph that Mary was following any sure guidance. If she had been sure, she would already have been on her way. He was anxious though himself. He would have been less uncertain, but he would never have the intuitive understanding of Jesus that Mary had. He must try to make up for it with extra care; he and Mary would go back.

They returned to the city. Worried and anxious, they found Jesus, and drew him away with them. Jesus too became worried. He was surprised that his own action should have caused distress. He would talk later with Joseph, to whom he could always explain things. With his mother, it was different. The place for explanations, as about Rachel being Jezebel, was when Mary did not know some fact. The reason for his staying on in the great synagogue had been something that she would have to *understand*. He spoke to her quietly: "Mary, holy mother, I was about our Father's business." He knew that forgiveness was his, unasked, and hoped that she also understood.

The childhood of Jesus had come to an end.

Book III

The Eldest Son

19

The Older Brother

The family was well established in Nazareth. They were no longer suffering the swings of fortune that tore them from their moorings and then swept them back again. Imperial Rome was far away, not wholly beneficent, and at this time not particularly malign. Some Jews there were who whispered of armed revolt, the "politicos" like those of Mary's earlier years, always on the lookout for the daring or the desperate. There was perhaps a re-awakening of interest in the interpretation of the Jews' religion. There was that strange group, the Essenes, who lived away from town and city, and preached brotherly love and tolerance. There were great teachers in Jerusalem itself, some of whom would ever remember the visit of Jesus and the youthful John. But what would you? There were ever rumours of new dawns, and Jerusalem in general believed that the right way was in the observance of their ancient religious laws, with meticulous attention to every detail.

These wider considerations were hardly in the thoughts of Mary and Joseph. As the parents of a large family, they had plenty to occupy themselves with in the demands of the daily round. The children, they discovered, never stayed the same. One child would be happy, another had encountered disaster, and what was disaster one day was a joke the next. There was barely enough time for Mary and Joseph to pause and reflect on the whole purpose of their striving—to lead their own lives in accordance with the will of God, and by their own lives give an example to their children. Might they all ever be faithful.

By the time Jesus was seventeen, there were seven children in the family, the last four born in Nazareth. Careful James (born in Egypt) was fifteen, and both the older boys were doing a full day's work with their father. James had always been the cautious one; he was the one who had *enjoyed* counting the sheep up at his uncle's farm, while Jesus had explored the hills. Rachel, two years old when they left Egypt, was now thirteen and a tempestuous thirteen at that, her eyes flashing like those of Uncle Reuben's wife Rebecca, whom she greatly admired. The contrast between the careful James and the more dashing Rachel was being repeated in the next two. The girl who came next, called Esther, had been *special* as the first girl to be born to them in Nazareth. Where Rachel was tempestuous, Esther by the age of nine was quiet, and best of all liked helping her mother at home.

Simeon, now seven, and *special* as the first boy of the family to be born in Nazareth, was happiest out on the hills around Uncle Benjamin's.

Mary wondered if the last two would fall into the same pattern. Joseph was now four. He was the one, Jesus had said, who was *special* in having the same name as their father. Last of all came a boy three years younger still. The boys had wanted, for no very obvious reason, to call him Judas, while Rachel, seeing that he was a big baby, wanted to call him Goliath. She had wept bitterly when she had been overruled, in favour of a name of one of their ancestors…Amos. Mary remembered that Rachel had also wept when her younger sister was called Esther, which she declared was a nicer name than her own.

There was work in plenty and surely the work of the Lord, within the family. Mary often thought back to the time when the only members of the family within her reach—perhaps the only ones still alive—had been Joseph and the three children, when her neighbours had been the wayward Vashti with the disreputable mother. Now, they were in the middle of the ramifications of a happy Jewish family. As well as their own children, there were Grandfather, and Benjamin and all his family up at the farm, and Reuben and Rebecca and all their relations in Capernaum, and Joseph's ageing Uncle Amos, not to mention regular news from old Cousin Elizabeth and her son John. As for friends and neighbours, many a "hurted" child was brought in to be tended by Mary's skilful fingers, and so many friends came to seek advice from Joseph that it was as well for the family income that his two older sons were working with him.

Not everything always went smoothly, even though the troubles were not great. There was, for example, the trouble they had for a while over James. James at fifteen was proving an excellent and very promising workman, and would stay at his work when his father, and indeed Jesus as well, would have gone off to see someone and stayed talking. James was beginning to feel that an unfair burden was being placed on him; why did Jesus not have to do what he was doing? Why did his parents let Jesus go off somewhere, like that time in the Temple, while he, James, carried on working? Joseph and Mary talked over the problem, and prayed that James might come to realise his own value instead of envying his brother. Not surprisingly, it was Jesus who did something to convince James. As the three older children sat with their parents one evening, Rachel being in one of her quiet and loving moods, Jesus said he had a story to tell them. Jesus was a good storyteller, so they were all ready to listen.

"There was a man," said Jesus, "who had quite a large estate and many servants," (not like us, thought his audience) "and he had two sons. When they grew up, the younger one wanted to travel away, so he asked his father for his share, which the father gave him. And then," said Jesus dramatically, "he went off to a foreign country, and he *spent* all the money that his father had worked so hard to get, and he made a lot of greedy false friends. And then the great river failed to flow," (echoes of Egyptian folk-tales, thought Joseph) "and everywhere there was poverty, and the young man, all alone in a foreign country—all his so-called friends had run off and left him—had to steal food from the pigs. So what did he do?" Dramatic pause. "He thought to himself, I will go back to my own father, and he will let me be his bond-servant. He went back, and his father forgave him, and we can all imagine what a lovely party they had that night."

This seemed a pleasant enough little tale, but it was only the introduction to what Jesus was really trying to say. He went on. "They were having a wonderful time, and making quite a lot of noise," (Rachel clapped her hands as she saw herself there) "and then—the older son, who had been away working hard all that day, under a hot sun in a distant field, came back. He wanted to know what was going on. When he found out, instead of being glad, he was jealous. He thought it meant that his father didn't love him, and he turned away, with tears in his eyes, and stumbled out into the darkness."

Jesus paused, for he wanted to see if James had understood. He looked at his younger brother with warmth and admiration, and the next thing was that it was James who was heard saying, "It isn't always the older brother who is jealous. But wasn't he silly not to realise how much their father depended on him?" A customer arrived, late though it was, and Jesus gently pressed his father back into his chair, while James went out to see to the man.

James' jealousy did not end at that very moment, but Mary noticed that from then on things became better, and Joseph and the two boys (the three men, Mary began to think) came into a unity that was to last the rest of their lives. Mary also noticed, as she thought over the story, that a good many of Jesus' stories were beginning to carry the same message—that it was wrong for people to be envious of someone else's good fortune, when the Lord had provided out of his bounty for everyone.

The next member of the family to cause concern to Mary was Rachel, and Mary confided in Jesus. The younger Esther was a quiet, considerate little girl, who enjoyed working alongside her mother, but Rachel was tempestuous and forgetful. Could Jesus make up another of his stories, something that would show Rachel she ought to think about other people a bit more? Jesus promised to try, and the occasion came when he had to escort his sister on a promised visit to their Uncle Reuben's house in Capernaum.

When they returned, it was to confess to his mother that he had failed. He had prepared what he thought would be an appropriate story, about a marriage feast, and how the five girls who were wise and provident had taken extra oil to keep their lamps burning, and the five careless ones had not and so were shut out of the feast. This seemed to Mary a very suitable story. What, she asked, had gone wrong? "Well, Ro-li-ma," Jesus explained, "I told her the story, and then I asked her which of the groups she thought she would be with. She said that as she intended to be the bride, she would have got in anyway, and in any case James would have made certain that she had enough oil. And if anyone was likely to be late or unsuitably dressed, it was me; not, she said that that was your fault." Jesus grinned. Rachel seemed to have summed up the family pretty well. Perhaps they should have been thinking of an adventurous way ahead for his sister rather than correcting her mistakes.

Other stories reached Mary from the visit to Capernaum. Jesus had spent much of his time beside the sea, talking with the boatmen, some of them distant cousins. Jesus was supposed to have shown them where the best fishing was. Jesus had rescued some fishermen when their boat had capsized. When asked about it, Jesus agreed that he had helped the men; he said it was simply that they had panicked, and he also reminded his mother that he was the only one who could swim—he had tried to teach the boys, but they wouldn't trust to the water. They had not had a Vashti to drop them in early enough!

It was not surprising that Jesus, always one to enjoy the company of others, and yet ever deeply thoughtful, had become one of the leading young men in the area. Joseph and Mary wondered if they ought to make opportunities for him to go away, somewhere where he might learn and experience more. Mary went to consult her father, as she had so often done. She remembered how she had come and asked him how to tell Jesus about his parentage, and indeed, before that, how to acquaint Joseph with it.

This time, the old man thought carefully, and then asked which had been the happy years in the young man's life. This was an easy question to answer. Rapidly she recounted them. Jesus had been too tiny of course to be bothered over the dreadful flight from Bethlehem, and the Egyptian years had been very happy for him, even though the food was a trifle unusual. Then he had the wonderful years after they had come back to Nazareth, with so much time up in the hills and with Grandfather. He had had good visits to the Passover, including the time when that had worried his parents when he had stayed on. He greatly liked being with John, the son of Elizabeth, whom he met in Jerusalem. He enjoyed working now with his father. The trouble with James had quite passed, and it was thanks to brother James that in this last year or two he had had more opportunity for going out and about. Mary could not say that any year had had more than a passing unhappiness for Jesus. In that case, said her father, the time has not yet come for him to go away; he is fine, and unspoilt, and his vision is undimmed; he is, perhaps, to be a leader of man, but as yet he is only in the making. The Lord is not to be hurried.

They both thought of the sufferings that the old man had been through. Mary hoped that Jesus might be spared such, but she could not have prayed for this. Their lives were in the Lord's hands.

20

Sadness

THE TRANQUIL FAMILY years passed. Children grew up, and the time came for marriages. When Jesus was twenty-four, the whole family went up for the Passover. It was the first time for Mary that there was much of sadness in the visit.

Nicodemus met them, as he usually did now, on their arrival. He had the glad news that the innkeeper from Bethlehem and his wife Hannah were for once at the Passover. Many messages had passed between the families, but Mary and Joseph were working folk, and Hannah and her husband ever pressed with business. It was the first time they had all been together since the birth of the baby in the stable. Question and answer poured out, thanks and congratulations on both sides.

They looked admiringly at the smiling figure of Jesus. Hannah only just stopped herself from saying, "How he has grown!" Nicodemus had told them the success stories. Now Hannah told them of some of the tragedies, still fresh in her mind after more than twenty years. The poor young shepherd, she said, poor man.

Mary waited, ready to blame herself for not having asked Nicodemus earlier. What had happened? It was that the man's young wife, after—after it had happened—had taken ill and died. Of course the shepherd could have married again, a fine young man like that, but he had gone out of his wits. He had not died; he lived still, howling and insane, with others like him in the desolate rocks out beyond Bethlehem. Bethlehem had tried to help him, but…to no avail…no avail… . No one could get near them.

For Mary, having learnt of the troubles of Bethlehem, and especially of the fate of that fine young man, it was already a troubled Passover. Jesus too had spent much of the time thinking about those afflicted with evil spirits. He had only briefly encountered any such, and he knew of the places where they were. Would the great readings and processions in Jerusalem bring help to these outcasts? All this, he talked over with his cousin John, who thought and prayed so much more than he did. (John fasted too, but that was a penance for the rich, not for the hard-up.) Jesus would have liked to question how the actions of some of the priests were helping the poor and outcast. What did John think? They talked long and uneasily. They found little answer from the foremost scribes and Pharisees. Were the priests ceasing to be prophets?

On the last evening of the Passover, Joseph, who now tired quickly, returned early to rest before the journey home. Mary went with Jesus to say goodbye to John and the widowed Elizabeth, and while the young men talked together, Elizabeth found courage to tell Mary what was on her mind. She started by congratulating Mary on the development of Jesus—a fine young man—and then went on, at times halting as she searched for the right words, "It is not only Jesus of whom you can be proud; you and Joseph have a fine family. My cousin Hannah would have rejoiced over them, just as, I am sure, that Zachariah would have been glad over our son John. Mary…you know that the time comes for all of us to face death. Sometimes it is for ourselves, and sometimes it is even more difficult, when we face it for those near to us. Mary, your own husband, Joseph, is ten years older than you are, and the time may, indeed the time probably *will* come when you will look to Jesus as the head of the family. I fear, cousin, that that time may come sooner than you think. Joseph is not strong. There was the accident to his leg when he was a child—and those strenuous years in Egypt… . Mary, I see so much difference in him this year."

Elizabeth went on to utter what she hoped might be words of comfort. "The Gentile sees a man as dead when his body is interred. To us, can a man die when his seed and his spirit are yet with us? Zachariah's presence has ever been with John and with me, and I think your father has ever felt the spirit of Hannah near him."

The final words meant little to Mary as the realisation came to her that what Elizabeth was telling her was true—Joseph could not expect to have long to live. Perhaps the other words would come back to her when they were needed, much, much later.

Jesus took her back to their lodgings. As she was downcast, he sought to make her laugh and brought out the childish word of encouragement, "festin alin", the words which had been the Latin for "make haste slowly" and which common parlance has turned into a dogged and cheery "persevere", "plod on". "Festin alin" must they all say after this Passover. "Festin alin, Mother." Mary tried to respond, and thought of what must now be done. The time had indeed come to think of the children marrying.

The first to be espoused was Rachel, now twenty-one years old. Jesus' story of the wise and foolish virgins had not got home to her, and Joseph's and Mary's ideas of an early marriage had come to naught. As Rachel grew up, she had shown more interest in going up to the Passover, or hearing what had been preached in the synagogue, or talking with Jesus when he returned with his tales of this or that acquaintance that he had made, often some foreigner. Mary, remembering the story of the older and the younger brother, was able to rejoice wholeheartedly in a daughter who was adventurous, as well as in Esther, the one who looked set to become someone's good wife. Rachel became espoused, having played rather more part in the proceedings than most Jewish young women did; so had Mary, long ago. There were great celebrations, and Mary was glad of the assistance of sister-in-law Rebecca, and at the end of the three days could only rejoice at Rachel's evident happiness. The espoused man, whose name was Ephraim, was well spoken and clever, quieter than one would have expected Rachel's choice to be, known to Nicodemus in Jerusalem. His parents lived in Corinth. He seemed to have much in common with Jesus. There was that about him that gave hints and promises of a wider destiny; it was Jesus who realised even sooner than his mother did, that this was a man who might be able to offer to Rachel the chance of wider horizons.

Joseph did not play much part in the celebrations. He tired so easily now and was glad that others could help Mary. Very soon after the celebrations, Joseph's own Uncle Amos, who had been ailing, died and for Joseph this was a grievous loss. It was true that one did not wish the life of a sick and ageing man prolonged, but it was an extra strain on Joseph. Mary was now remembering only too well the warning given her by her cousin Elizabeth.

The espousal of Rachel had reminded Joseph and Mary, if they needed reminding, that James should marry soon. There had been plenty of families ready to encourage their daughters to look at James—such a reliable workman, and a good and loving son. Perhaps it was the very number and suitability of brides that had made them postpone making arrangements. Now, with Joseph ageing before their eyes, the espousal must be arranged. There should be an alliance with a neighbouring family, well thought of and well established. The bride to be was the second child and the oldest daughter, two years younger than James, and a good capable young woman. It was all very suitable. Her name was Abigail.

Somehow no one thought of arranging a marriage for Jesus. Had he himself thought about it? If he had, had he rejected the idea of children being born when no one could say who their father's father had been? In any case, he must now take his share with Mary in helping the family in what was becoming a year of great troubles. It was not only that Joseph's strength was failing, Mary's father too was ill, and it soon became clear that Grandfather had little time to live.

The old man summoned as many of the family as could come. He had, he said, reached the allotted age of three score years and ten; he had had such great cause for thankfulness, great cause. When Hannah had been taken from him, her spirit had yet seemed to remain with them. Reuben and Benjamin had always been good sons. When Mary, dear Mary, had been with child, Joseph had accepted her. After the dreadful years of their absence, they had returned in safety. They must remember, as he had done, that the Lord would continue to bless them if they remained ever faithful.

He died peacefully, his children and his children's children about him.

Joseph had only a short time to live now. He could not quite muster the serenity with which the two older men had seen their deaths approaching. He would have liked to have seen grandchildren. Then he remembered with great gratitude all that his life had owed to Mary—Mary, the girl who had so much enjoyed the freedom of the hills, Mary as the steadfast wife bearing the first children so uncomplainingly in strange uncomfortable places. He recalled the happy years after their return, golden years of promise and of harvest. What message could he leave as he said goodbye to her? He thought again of Jesus, Mary's child, who had brought so much happiness into their lives together. Yes, there was one final thing to repeat that might help Mary, though she might already realise it; he roused himself to say to her that the future of Jesus would not always be in the family, but it was Jesus himself who would know when to leave. Mary need not worry, Mary must not worry. After Joseph had said this, his weary body lapsed into sleep. During the night, while Mary and the children gathered round, his unwilling spirit left.

The year that had started with talk of marriages and hope of children to come, ended with the deaths of the two people who had meant so much. Mary tried to remember the things that her father had told them. He had gone through a time of despair, he had said, and then come out of it. *Festin alin*. One did not give up. One remembered those who were smaller and weaker, in that was one's shield. Uncle Amos and her father and Joseph had been good men, their lives showing obedience to God. For her now, there were Jesus and the other children, and one found help by praying and by looking to their future, and also by remembering those times when her own vision had failed and Joseph had had to overrule her.

For Jesus, his immediate path was clear. Soon James would be married and would come to take his place as the head of the family; now he, Jesus, must take the place of Joseph and share his mother's duties. He wept as he remembered that the years of Joseph's unfailing kindness had ended. Joseph had risked his life and his reputation for him, Jesus; a man could do no more.

It was children, as it so often is, who brought Mary out of her time of sadness. Benjamin's children wanted to show her the new animals (some of whom were actually, said their father, the descendants of a ram called Jacob that had once belonged to their Auntie Mary). And would she come and tell them if she liked the new stones they had put round the well? They had planned it out with Grandfather, they said, and it made them cry to think he wasn't there. But he had told them that you had to finish what you started. Mary was glad to get the first visits to the farm over; once there, she found that in Benjamin's children she had an audience who wanted to hear more about their grandfather, and even their grandmother. Her visits to the farm became more frequent. Her sixteen-year-old son, Simeon, often went too. Jesus was now the head of the family, with much family business to see to. True, there were some in Nazareth who murmured when he spent so much time with visitors and acquaintances from outside. It was almost, they said, as if one's family was not enough. As a young man it had been good that Jesus should show fire and dash and be aware of a wide, wide world, but the job of a head of a family was to be with that family. James, the second son was a very reliable person. It was good that his marriage would be so soon.

Abigail's parents, like Joseph, were ones to plan ahead, and neither Jesus nor Abigail's father saw any reason for delay. The prospects of James were assured. Abigail would be welcomed by Mary, and would gradually take over the work in the house, until such time, of course, as she was with child, when it would be well that there were other women in the house to do the work. The wedding would be a fine one. None of the girls would be likely to come to that wedding unprepared, no guest likely to be without proper wedding garments (except perhaps Jesus). The sadness of not having Joseph there to make the arrangements was partly offset by the pleasure of Abigail's parents, who were glad to see their daughter about to become the wife of the excellent James. They were also glad that the older woman in the house would be Mary; it was not always easy for a bride.

Quite unexpectedly, Rachel's marriage took place first. She had not seemed impatient; she had expected that James would marry first, and she had been contented enough in playing a very small part in what was still her family. Mary was pleased, and it must be said not a little surprised, at the patience of her older daughter. Rachel had not been one to put up with anything quietly, not from the time that she had woken up on their first night out of Egypt and roused even the donkeys with her yells. Ephraim must have some special magic that gave her willingness to wait. Jesus thought that the special magic might lie in the young man's vision of their future. It was not for Rachel, as it was for Abigail or little sister Esther, to see a whole future in some well-established house not far from the rest of the family.

Ephraim returned unexpectedly with news that caused Jesus to persuade his mother that Rachel's wedding must take place immediately. His mother was not to worry that Rachel would be going so far away; if she was to go with her husband to Ephesus or even Rome, she was going to be one who travelled, and one who travelled was one who came back on visits. The wedding was prepared in haste. Ephraim's father did not come, only his mother and an aunt. There were fewer guests, and less magnificent wedding garments than Mary would ever have expected for the wedding of Rachel. Even the wine ran out, and it was the great happiness of the bridal pair that saved the situation—and the way Jesus made it an occasion for a joke. He had made them fill jars with water, and then solemnly declared it to be wine, and the guests had laughed at this, and been merrier than at many a more costly wedding. It recalled to Mary that happy journey to Jerusalem when she had posed as Grandma and her father as the young singer. Jesus had indeed helped to make his sister's wedding a memorable occasion.

Then came the wedding of James and Abigail. Not on this occasion would important relations be absent, and certainly the wine did not run out. James played his part with an assurance that promised well for the future of those who might be dependent on him. Abigail looked less self-assured than Rachel had done, and Mary hoped it was not spiteful to assume that this was a lesson Abigail's mother had taught her—a bride should not appear too eager. Mary was certain that Abigail was as joyful as Rachel had been, and equally well prepared for *her* future.

Mary already felt that this was one more step to the time when Jesus would leave them. She could not have said why she was so certain of this.

For the present, Jesus was the head of the family, with a concern, sometimes concealed under a joke, for each member. Abigail must have time to settle in; James must take more time away from work; he, Jesus, would finish some of the work ordered. He, Jesus, would also take an opportunity to talk with "young" Joseph. Joseph was nearly thirteen; he worked in the carpenter's shop. He slightly resented the appellation "young" and felt that in some ways he was going to be a better workman than James. "Look, Jesus," he said (it was always easier to talk to Jesus than it was to James), "look at this; it's a tiny piece of olive, but if I give it a twist *here* and a bit of polish *there*—see, I can make it into the image of a fish, with a coin in its mouth. Only James will say that it's a waste of time, and that it should be wood for kindling." It is ever thus, thought Jesus, that the artist will look at the man of business. To the young Joseph, he spoke of the value of the artist, of the eye that sees what ordinary people and men of business do not notice. They all needed the artists among them. At the end of the afternoon he mentioned, as if casually, that the greatest test for the seeing eye is to understand another human being. Understanding James, for example, could be quite a hard thing to do, and might need a real artist to tackle it.

It was after that that James began to find how much he could depend on young Joseph.

The Sabbaths were times for prayer and thought, and to Mary it seemed that Jesus had many of her father's ways. James too contributed, and brought back from the synagogues the words of their own or visiting rabbis. In Benjamin's home, up on the hill, and in their own and in so many good Jewish homes, the ritual prayers were said, the verses read and treasured. Jesus was almost being tempted into feeling that this was to be his rightful destiny, looking after his family here in Nazareth. Would it be right to leave his mother, or his youngest brother, the ten-year-old Jesse? Hard-working domestic Esther was ready to pledge her troth with a nearby young Samuel, but nothing should be attempted, in spite of her wishes, until he and Mary and James were satisfied about the young man's prospects; would it be right to leave to James the job of standing up against a determined younger sister? For Simeon of course, there was no need to worry; his love of the hills had already made him virtually a member of his Uncle Benjamin's family, and a welcome companion to Mary on her visits there. Might it not be better that he, Jesus, should stay here? Why move into a wider, and more uncertain world? The world indeed came to you, with visitors and passing traders, and one's own journeys to Jerusalem to the Passover. The temptation was there. Man does not live by bread alone, but what if the bread is what a man is obtaining for his own family?

It was on one of the visits to the Passover that a small incident occurred that reminded Jesus that he could not always stay as the head of a prospering family in a small town in Galilee. Mary was not sure exactly what it was that had happened. Jesus told her that he had helped some men carry a cripple up to a high place where the man could see properly all that was going on. And the Pharisees had said that it defiled the Temple for someone who was a sinner to be within the wall, as well as being unnecessary work for the people who carried him, it being the Sabbath. When Mary heard about it, she wondered how they had been so sure that the man was a sinner.

22

Second and Third Temptations

RACHEL RETURNED, UNEXPECTEDLY, to visit her old home. She was well, she had a baby, as they had already heard, and Ephraim was with her. She had a look of contentment, though she was thinner, and a little bit careworn. The childish prettiness had gone, and there was an expression now that wavered between thoughtfulness and watchfulness. She talked with Esther and asked about Esther's own marriage prospects. "You must tell my absent-minded brothers to get on with the arrangements," she joked, although neither Jesus nor James could really have been accused of being absentminded. She admired the work young Joseph was doing… "All right, I won't call you young Joseph any more, for I can see by your work that you are no longer a child." She went up to the farm, and left the precious baby with Benjamin's wife, while she tramped round with her brother Simeon...a performance quite unlike that of the Rachel of earlier days. It was of course Mary who noticed that Rachel was asking all the questions and listening to all the answers, she was not giving opportunities for anyone to ask her questions. Mary confined her own questions to innocuous ones about the baby's progress, and made herself a listener in case Rachel wanted to tell more.

After a day or two it was Ephraim who made an opportunity for an uninterrupted talk with Jesus. Perhaps this was why he had come. Jesus, he said, must have guessed that he, Ephraim, was not merely a man of business. Jesus had been going about, had not stayed all the time in Nazareth. Jesus himself had many contacts, and he must already have realised that...that things might be changing, coming to a head. The ruler, Herod Antippas, was hated both for himself and as a puppet of Rome. Now could be the time to gather together those people, already feeling like...like the existing group did...and prepare the great insurrection which should leave the country free again. Free...our own masters again... free, as we have the right and the ability to be. Ephraim was a clever speaker, and sincere. He knew when to declaim, and when to drop his voice to a quiet confidentiality. What they needed, he said, were men of vision and men who would be trustworthy. He had already heard from his acquaintances of the views of Jesus. Jesus, he was sure, was on their side. And it was already beginning to show that the words of Jesus could sway many people. Ephraim allowed himself to laugh as he said that in faraway

Corinth they had heard how Jesus had made the water taste like wine! And, seriously, the time was ripe now for action; Ephraim's own business interests were little more than a cover for the political work he was doing, and he knew, he *knew* what the situation was. If Jesus would join them, he would at once have a position of influence. Might not Jesus be *the* man they were waiting for, the man of the future...and what could he not do then, with his country once more the leader and not the slave of Egypt and Assyria, even of Rome itself? It was a glittering prospect that Ephraim laid out. And it was not impossible. Ephraim was accurate in his impressions, already with a wide knowledge, and yet as wholehearted and sincere as Jesus himself. It must have been a tempting offer.

The next morning Rachel and her baby and Ephraim left. There were many cries of "Farewell" and "Come back soon", though Mary was surprised to hear Jesus say, "Goodbye...Satan." She wondered what it meant. What it did seem to mean was that there was another piece of family business to be transacted immediately. If she and James concurred, the marriage of Esther could now take place. Esther herself had long been ready to encourage the attentions of a young member of the community named Samuel. Although this name was of good omen to them, as Esther herself had more than once pointed out, her brothers had waited till the young man had established himself. Satisfied on this point (Samuel now had steady work on a nearby farm), Jesus was ready to arrange the marriage. He thought to himself that if he had yielded to one particular Satan, it would have been

James who would have been the head of the family and arranging this. So quite soon there was another happy occasion in Mary's family, a well-arranged and well-attended wedding, with a stalwart bridegroom and a capable young bride, and as it were a chorus of nieces and nephews and little and big cousins. For Esther there was no pretence of being a reluctant bride…the girl, noticed Mary, positively *smirked*. How happy Joseph would have been; so much that he had worked and hoped for was coming to pass.

For Jesus, this happy family gathering stood out in stark contrast to the glittering visions conjured up by Ephraim. Need a man seek further than to serve his own family? The first temptation was still strong.

The next year, there was another visit to the Passover. During this, yet a third temptation, even greater than the second, was laid in front of Jesus. The family had not accompanied him to Jerusalem. Abigail had just given birth to the first much longed for child, and Mary would stay with her. Even their cousin John was not in Jerusalem, for he was at home—it looked as if Elizabeth had not long to live. Jesus was therefore by himself: he was met, as usual, by Nicodemus, and then taken to meet someone else. This was someone of importance, said Nicodemus, who wanted to meet Jesus; he would have liked to meet John too, only John was not there this year.

Afterwards, Jesus could never remember being told the names of the man, and he never knew what happened afterwards to the man. There were times when he wondered if he should have listened more obediently to what this man had said. The man, repeated Nicodemus, was someone of importance, and he went away and left them together. Jesus wondered if the man was a disciple of the Essenes, and warmed to him at once.

They sat for a little while in courteous silence together, and then the man started talking. He spoke first of trifles, the silver-grey of the wings of the doves which yet flashed black against the blue of the heavens, the aroma of incense and the memories it conjured up, the changing sounds of the wind as it whispered through the olive trees at Gethsemane or hurtled itself against the solid walls of the Temple. How much had happened here in the Temple! The man spoke of Solomon, and of Nehemiah, and quoted some of the well-known verses about the rebuilding of the Temple. Jesus, he remarked, did not need to be told that the important rebuilding had not been in stone but in the hearts of men. Had the time come again for a rebuilding of their Temple? Man had forgotten at times to listen to what God was saying to them; even some of the priests had begun to judge by outward appearances—like the priests who had harangued Jesus, two years ago, was it, when the poor sick man had been helped up on to the eastern rampart. It surprised Jesus that the incident should have been noted.

The man's voice continued, warm and appealing. There were men of vision even now in the circles of the priests, and it behoved—other men of vision—to join with them. The outer Temple could be destroyed, and yet the inward Temple could be rebuilt; what an opportunity it would be for all concerned…an even greater opportunity for one brought up as a working man outside the ranks of the Temple. What did Jesus think of the offer? This was an offer. Come, was this a time in their history to hesitate? Would he not join them?

It took Jesus some minutes to realise the prize he was being offered; he was being offered a place among the great ones of his nation, the scribes and Pharisees and teachers of the Temple, he, Jesus, the son of an unknown man and a girl from the hills of Galilee. Aghast, he went away, unable to give the man an immediate answer. Was this what God was telling him to do?

He stumbled as if blind through the streets, and presently found himself in a part of the city that he hardly knew. A woman swayed into him enticingly, only to be herself pulled away by a drunken soldier. Jesus realised what part of the city he had come to. He watched a couple of pickpockets play the old trick; one pushed against the arm of a well dressed passer-by, while the other took the man's purse. It was here, realised Jesus, here and among these people, that the inward Temple had to be rebuilt. He noticed later that his own scrip had gone.

He returned and found Nicodemus waiting for him. Would Nicodemus please tell his friend that the answer must be no. If the people concerned remained true to what he had heard, God would surely send someone, but someone else, to accomplish their task. For him, the answer was no. Nicodemus looked thoughtful, remembering the time when he had succeeded in making a mother whisk a baby away from impending death. It was not always healthy, sometimes not even safe, to turn down offers from the great ones of the Temple. Was Jesus condemning himself? Nicodemus tried to shake off this feeling. An important person himself now, he must not allow himself to indulge in melodramatic thoughts.

Nicodemus returned to the Temple. Jesus left the Passover early. Their ways no longer lay together.

23

Interlude

JESUS, AND MARY too, knew that their time together would now be short. There should be a little time for them to be alone together without the cares of the family. Mary, with more time for herself than at any moment in the last thirty years, wanted to visit her older brother Reuben in his own home. Although there had been much visiting, it had been largely by the children, or by Rebecca. Jesus felt he could leave family business quite safely with James. He would conduct Mary to Capernaum, and for him and Mary there would be this little time when they could still be together, could talk, reminisce, and enjoy the journeying, as well as visiting another branch of the family.

Arrived in Capernaum, Mary looked at her sister-in-law's home; she was pleased with what she saw. Reuben probably no longer knew whether his wife had hair as black as a raven's wing or tangled wisps of grey, but it could be seen that the two relied on each other for solid and satisfactory support. Although the house was wealthier than either theirs in Nazareth or Benjamin's up on the hill, there was the same attention to fulfilling one's duties, the same observance of the religion of their people. Mary could be satisfied with what she saw. Her father could have sat here at ease, pleased with his son Reuben. So perhaps Jesus would now take Mary to some of the places that he had already visited in Capernaum and so often told her about.

Like Jesus, she was aware that a change was coming in the household in Nazareth. It would have been exceedingly pleasant if Jesus could have remained there, but she did not feel that it was God's will to use her eldest son in this way. She did not know of the details of what had been, for Jesus, real temptations. Like Melchior, she sensed the inner meanings, and she was not awaiting what might be some great opportunity for Jesus, or rather, not so much an opportunity for him to excel over others, but a demand that he had to meet. It would not be a chance to become important that would call Jesus, nor would it have occurred to *her* to want this: there would be some place, some spot, where he would be able to give some help to others. He was good with people who were ill, and sometimes he found the word that seemed to encourage them. There would be work for him to do.

They walked beside the lake unhurried, at ease. "Mother," asked Jesus, "have you noticed that

Grandfather never seems to have left us? The children talk as if he were still there. You hear Simeon tell Jesse to do something "the way Grandpa tells us!" Mary agreed. "When I think of my father," she said, "it often reminds me of the visit of the wise men when you were born. Their visit was short, and their spirit has always stayed with me, as I am sure it did with Joseph." She always used a past tense when speaking of Joseph. It was his bodily presence that had meant so much, to all of them. He had done so many things for them. To herself, she was thinking that Jesus too was one of those whose spirits remain when the physical presence has gone. She gave a start as she realised that what she was thinking could apply if Jesus died before she did; she had only meant that she would feel him close in spirit when he went away to fulfil his calling.

She turned her attention to the sights around them, and listened eagerly to what Jesus told her about Capernaum. The big boat there belonged to their friend, Simon Peter—a big fellow, who would hardly have fitted into a small boat. The next one belonged to Rebecca's relations, the Zebedees. Out there, on the left, was where that other boat had capsized, when he had helped to rescue the men in it. The story now being told, said Jesus, was that he had told the *winds* to be still, when all that he had really done was to tell those silly *men* to be calm and not to panic. "You understand that, Ro-li-ma?" (He used the old nickname for Mary.)

The visit over, they returned to Nazareth. Mary enjoyed walking the hills almost, but not quite, as if she was still a young woman. It had been a good visit. It was good now to be home again, she went to look at baby Matthew and hushed a fretful whimper. How fine had been the hills. The Lord had been and ever would be a tower of strength to her, and to all who trusted in him.

Jesus found occasion to talk with his sister-in-law, Abigail, who was looking uneasy. One would have thought that it was from her that the fretful whimper had come. "Abigail," said Jesus, "what will thee call thy daughter?" "Naomi," she answered, and then looked with surprise at Jesus. "How didst thou know? I am not yet with child." Jesus laughed. "Dear prudent sister-in-law, do thee not plan ahead? Did you not think, in choosing the name of your firstborn, that "James" and "Matthew" would slide easily off the tongues of customers?" Abigail again looked at Jesus with surprise; what a question to ask, of course they had thought of this; it would have been most improvident not to. "And why," said Jesus, "with all this looking ahead, which is proper to thee and James, art thou so uneasy? Our Lord shall be a strength to you as to all of us."

Abigail confessed. What was worrying her was Mary, and Mary's position. Mary was getting older, old enough to take more rest, instead of always being about, here and up on the hill, helping the children and everyone who called on her. She was not a young woman any more. So that was the trouble, mused Jesus. Mary did not fit into the picture that had been prepared for Abigail, probably by Abigail's own mother, of an older woman who would have to be waited on by a devoted daughter-in-law. He decided that he would have to tell them all another story before he went away, which might help his excellent, though unimaginative sister-in-law to see more clearly Mary's place. He told Abigail that all would be well but that he had another story for them. Before he left, he must help Abigail to understand Mary's place.

There was never any lack of an audience when Jesus said he was going to tell a story. The family gathered when the day's work was done. This story, said Jesus, was about the master of a great estate, the estate he had once told James about, with the two brothers. The father was dead now, and one of the brothers was the master now, and a very good master. (As to which of the brothers it was, that was quite another story...some other time, perhaps.) The master was going away on a long journey, and he entrusted his money to certain of his servants; he gave one thousand talents to one, and five hundred to another, and to a third, two hundred and fifty. The first two were clever and honest, as of course the master knew, and of course they used their master's money well, and had doubled it by the time he got back. He was pleased with them, and he rewarded them, for they had done even better than he had expected. Now about the third servant (Jesus shook his head ruefully), he was not as clever as the other two. The master knew this, which was why he only gave him two hundred and fifty talents. It was very sad, but the silly fellow let himself be talked into being afraid; he just *hid* the money, and when the master came back, there it was, the same amount that he had been given to start with. You can all see what I am telling you—wasn't it a pity that the other two, who were strong and clever, hadn't tried to help and encourage the third one?"

Jesus looked straight at Abigail. "What great talents you and James have. You must ever be ready; one day it may be the will of our Father who is in Heaven to call you to some greater service." Jesus was hardly foreseeing James's position as a central figure in some new church, yet to be, in Jerusalem…he had not even started to think of himself as a great leader who would be followed. It was just that he was aware of James' talents, and wanted others to be so too.

The next morning he spoke more directly to his sister-in-law. "Abigail, there is one more thing that I was telling you last night. You must try to think of our mother as if she were the servant who only had two hundred and fifty talents; you yourself, who have the five hundred, will grow in strength and wisdom, and you will *encourage* her to use her talents; it will not be difficult. But you could be the one to try with well-meant and ill-placed kindness to bury them." It was not usually so necessary to explain exactly what the stories meant, but the capable Abigail was one to like clear instructions. Jesus then added that he would be going away soon, which, as he had expected, was a surprise to her. She had had no idea. She asked if he was going to Ephraim. Perhaps his sister-in-law was cleverer than he had credited her with being.

He was content. The family was in the capable hands of James and Abigail. Mary, who in his eyes possessed talents beyond price, would not be fretted towards an unnatural quiet. For him, a call would soon come, a call and not a temptation. He was ready, his last duties to the family accomplished.

Book IV

Ministry and Resurrection

24

Baptism by John

RUMOURS AND NEWS sometimes travelled swiftly, at times seemed to seep away into the desert sands. All heard when Elizabeth was ill and when she died, Elizabeth was remembered as one whose great happiness had been the bearing of a son to the ageing Zachariah. Her memory would ever be blessed. Mary thought of the time that she had spent with Elizabeth before their children were born, and of how they had talked of her own. mother, Hannah, lovely in face and spirit. She was sure that kind good Elizabeth had died peacefully, and would have liked to hear what her final words and prayers had been. Perhaps John would come. She did not think that the news would affect her own family.

John did not come. News did not come. To Mary it

seemed most likely that he should have gone to the Temple, there to follow, and in time even to surpass his father, the upright Zachariah. Then came the news. John had gone up to the High Priest. John had been rejected. John had shaken the dust of Jerusalem off his feet. He was in the desert. He was preaching a new vision.

Jesus knew, as clearly as if the clouds had parted and a bird cried out the words, that he too must go. He and John had always been close and this was the call. He said goodbye to his mother. "Your spirit will ever be with me." He went away in the night.

The next day young Joseph left, work unfinished, and with a brief word of farewell to his mother, he went to follow Jesus.

When Jesus left, Mary knew that he had gone to start on the next task of his life. He would join John, perhaps they would do something together; theirs might be some great mission, or else something quite simple. She prayed that if they became important (that in itself was an odd idea), they would withstand the temptations that come with high position. She prayed too for their safety. When she would see Jesus again, or in what circumstances, must depend on things outside her own life. For her, the years of daily companionship were over.

She thought long. That the work of John and Jesus would bring them into danger, she guessed. It might involve loneliness for them. It might call Jesus to some distant clime, or he might be distant only in the sense that he was at his work on the other side of the country; he might be heading for some great task in Jerusalem, to be seen by his family once a year, and then at a distance. That they would ever be in his thoughts and prayers, she need not doubt. She must be steady herself for the time ahead, and try to support his calling by herself being faithful to her own obligations. The life of the rest of the family must go on. She prayed that the Lord who had protected her and her husband in the past would now grant her the wisdom to fulfil any role she might yet have to play in the life of her eldest son as well as in the life of those around her.

It was not long before Joseph returned, a sadder, and perhaps a more experienced young man. Part of what had happened they had of course already heard by then…news of that kind travelled quickly. Some of the things that Jesus had done only came to them through Joseph. After the evening meal on Joseph's return, they gathered round him; Mary, James and Abigail, Simeon and young Jesse. Joseph told the whole story in a flat monotonous tone, quite unlike his usual emphatic utterances. He was seventeen years old, and usually loved to tell a story with great effect, just as Jesus did. Now, the event which would change all their lives was recounted in a dull even tone.

"When we heard about our cousin John and his great preaching," said Joseph, "I guessed that Jesus would go and join him. I remembered how Jesus always told us how important cousin John was, and that we should be ready to listen to him. I've always thought it was Jesus we should listen to. But when we heard that John had been in the desert praying and had come out and started preaching, I guessed Jesus would go and join him, and

I told Jesus that I was going to come too. You know that Jesus went in the night, without me, so I decided I would follow him. I thought I would go to Jerusalem first, and try and see Nicodemus and ask if he knew where Jesus was. I thought he would be with John. But when I got nearer to Jerusalem, everyone I met was talking about John, and there was no need to ask the way. Lots of them had already been out and seen him, and a lot more were on their way. So I went along with them. I was really looking for Jesus, and I couldn't see him anywhere. But there was John. There was John. I couldn't get anywhere near him there were so many people round him. So I thought I would wait till they had gone home. I went over to a little hill and sat down and ate the food I had, and while I sat there, I could see what was happening. There was a crowd of people, and there were all sorts of people. Some of them were people who were ill, who had been helped to get there. Some of them…I mean the ones who were well…went up to John and he baptised them.

"Every now and then he would stop and preach. He told us what dreadful sinners we were. I was quite a long way away, but I could hear every word he said. He said we must come and be baptised, and have our sins washed away, and he said that someone was coming who was more important than he was, much more important. He kept saying that, and that we must repent. Some of the people on the edge of the crowd were quite rough people, and I heard some of the others complaining that the rough ones hadn't any business to be there. There were important people too. There were some of the priests from the Temple. I thought they didn't like what was going on. There were some people near them who looked to me like sort of spies, the kind they say that are used by the palace.

"When it was evening, most of the crowd went away, and I wanted to go and ask cousin John if he had seen Jesus, but as soon as the people had gone, John went striding off. And he didn't look as if anyone could ask him anything. He was dreadfully thin. It made him look even taller than he used to. One man told me that John had been living quite rough out in the desert and he looked as if he had.

"Next day, it was the same again, only I saw Jesus coming. I was going to run up and embrace him, but there were quite a lot of people round him too. Then John saw him. John had been like—like an emperor before—telling everyone what to do and calling down wrath and blessings from the Lord. Only when he saw Jesus, he was quite different. He told everyone to be quiet. All the crowd went quiet, and everyone stopped moving, except Jesus of course, who went up to John, and John called out, "Blessed is the hour. Here is the man I told you about, whose very shoe I am unworthy to touch. This is the Master." But Jesus asked that John should baptise him. John looked as if he thought it should be the other way round, with Jesus baptising him. That's what I thought too. I know I would rather have followed Jesus, although he made John do the baptising. I don't know what happened after that, because the crowd all started talking and calling out again, and a whole lot more went and got baptised.

"I thought I would stay and be with Jesus after that, as I wanted to follow him.

"It was evening before I could get to him. He said that he had seen me in the crowd; I didn't know that he had. He made me come and have some food with him. He asked me, quite kindly, what I was doing there, and I said that I had come to follow him. I thought he would have been pleased. But he said that I was to come home again to go on with my father's business. He didn't exactly say that he didn't want me with him, and yet in a way he did. He said, and I still don't understand what he meant, but he said that others would be his brothers and his mother, and that not everyone, perhaps even in our own family, would understand how he had to go about his father's business. He said that it was not for me "to drink the same cup". A lot of them prayed together that evening, and I stayed with them, and in the morning I started home."

The family sat silent. Then James, now the head of the family, asked Mary if she would like to sit with them or would like to go early to her bed. Mary stayed. James, mindful of Mary rather than of himself, thought of Jesus, the brother whose vision was taking him to "other brothers and mother". Wherever it was he was going, he would need their hopes and prayers, in measure unexpected. Might the Lord give him, James, the understanding to help his mother and to guide the family of which he was now the head.

He wished he could have found the right words from the scriptures with which to comfort Mary. Grandfather would have known what to say. James repeated some of the words attributed to King David, and ended up rather lamely with the inappropriate motto from the Latin: "Festin Alin". *Festin alin,* persevere, was a much more prosaic expression than the occasion demanded. It brought a smile to his mother's face. Drinking the cup that Jesus drank would be, for her, helping his brothers to face their daily tasks now that Jesus was no longer there as the head of the family, no longer there except in spirit.

The first thing to do was to give some cheer to Joseph, whose attempt to be a follower of Jesus had failed. Abigail went out to prepare a meal, her contribution. James and Mary tried vainly to think of what to say. It was the fifteen-year-old Jesse who found the right approach. He addressed Joseph and explained how he, Jesse, had worked on the piece of carpentry unfinished by Joseph, but although he had tried, he had somehow not been able to finish it off properly. Would Joseph come and show him again how to do it? Yes, Joseph would. James, who had himself intended to finish off the work, looked with added respect at the young Jesse. Jesse had always been friendly, to one and all, but this gesture was showing a nice perception of the feelings of others. If Joseph's attempt to be a "fisher of men" had been rejected, he was at least being offered a useful path as the teacher of a younger brother.

25

Rejection by Galilee

THE NEXT YEARS were for Mary the years of waiting and watchfulness. Jesus had left his family and was embarking on the years of his ministry. For him there would now be "another family", a family that seemed, as news reached Mary, to encompass the whole world. For her, they were years when her path was likely to be a quiet one of tending "those smaller and weaker than oneself". As a mother, and a Jewish mother at that, she would have liked to do something that she could see was of some definite help to Jesus. As Mary, who had already seen visions on the hills before ever she left her childhood home, there was an awareness that she could only help Jesus by herself being in readiness for whatever served God's purpose. On that day long ago on her first journey to the Passover, she had talked to a child called John about obeying God's word. It was not always easy, as now, when for her it meant watching and waiting: what it was coming to mean to Jesus, she was almost afraid to think. Leaving the family must have been so hard, and that was only the start.

Just as there had been three temptations to assail Jesus, there were three...not perhaps temptations, but certainly hopes for her about what might happen to her son Jesus. The first temptation, or hope, had already passed. Like Jesus, she had hoped that the way would open for him to stay with her and with the family. How welcome had been the occasional visits of Jesus to the home of Uncle Benjamin, and would it not have been right for Jesus to see what would transpire for the future of Simeon, Simeon who so much fitted the life of the upland farmer? And James now, with the complete responsibility of the family business, always being called away to talk with customers, when he would rather have spent the time with Abigail and his infant son; how Jesus' presence would have helped. Joseph was becoming a good worker, thoughtful, and imaginative in a way that James would never be; how much Jesus would have been encouraging him. And how much she would have welcomed a word about the youngest of the family, Jesse, who seemed to follow in the footsteps of Jesus one week, and of James another.

The hope that Jesus might stay with his family had passed. It had never been something for which Mary would have felt it right to pray.

The second hope seemed reasonable enough. No sooner had Jesus left them than his fame became known. This was no humble position that he was filling. Far from anything that Mary had even envisaged, her son had become a man of whom many people spoke. Soon came the news that he was travelling towards Galilee, and with it, her second hope. His work might indeed lie in Galilee itself. For this she could pray.

Many and various stories reached them, of his teaching, of the crowds assembled beside the sea, of Jesus going out in a small boat from which to speak so that everyone who wanted could hear. And there were the stories too of great healing miracles, of lepers cured and sight restored. There was the miraculous healing of someone whom Rebecca and Reuben actually knew, mother to the wife of the big fisherman Simon called Peter. One moment she had laid in a fever, awaiting death. The same afternoon she had been up and about, looking after them all. All these stories, and many others, came to Nazareth, some true, some born of what someone thought someone else said they had seen. To Mary and the family the news sometimes seemed as if it could not possibly be true—was this man, whom so many people were following, the Jesus who had lived and worked with them? At other times, something he was reported as doing or saying was exactly the kind of thing they recognised.

John's teaching of "Repent" had been superseded by "The Kingdom of Heaven is here, all around you". Some of the sayings attributed to Jesus, Mary did not understand, but that was hardly surprising, so much had his stories always been directed to a particular hearer or hearers. Others seemed to her precisely the kind of thing that her father might have been saying: "The earth is the

Lord's and the fullness thereof"..."Lord, help us to forgive those whom we think are our enemies"..."deliver us from the evil that is in our own hearts"..."Blessed are the peacemakers". "Blessed are the peacemakers," thought Mary, was something Jesus had always acted on.

Some of the news that came was incomprehensible. There was, for example, the story that a herd of animals (valuable animals at that) had been driven into the sea by Jesus and drowned. This Mary rejected as impossible. Other reports that specially interested her were those of her son's curing the poor sick insane; how wonderful it would have been if the poor young shepherd from Bethlehem had survived till now and been restored to health by Jesus. That there were already signs of opposition from "the Temple" was not reported. Probably nobody noticed, except perhaps Jesus himself, and in any case it is the sudden and the miraculous that gets reported.

One piece of news that everyone could understand was that Jesus had selected a special group to be close to him. These would be the men to learn directly from him, his disciples. Mary could only marvel that the power of God had so shown itself, not merely in the choice of the twelve, but in the fact that these particular twelve, selected from the hundreds pressing around him, should have been accepted by the whole countryside. It was not only of "Jesus of Nazareth" now that men talked, it was of "Jesus and his disciples", and they had only been ordinary people. Mary rejoiced as she thought of all that Jesus was doing. Some people everywhere must have been feeling cast down by the teachings of the scribes and Pharisees, when in order to be good you had to keep each and every detail of a whole set of regulations; small wonder that many were being driven into failure and rebellion. The teaching of Jesus was that the Kingdom of Heaven was there, for everyone who tried to do the will of God and helped the poor and weak. Trying to do the will of God was something that everyone could do, and there was always someone smaller and weaker than yourself to be helped.

It seemed that the work of Jesus was centring round Capernaum and the Sea of Galilee. Might it not be that this was where he was to remain? To Mary, it came as something for which she might pray. Might it be that Jesus would find his life's task here in Galilee?

The reports that had reached them were as nothing to the impact made by the visit of one of the disciples. There was one who came and from the noise of his arrival, there might have been legion. There was the noise of his stamping feet, and a voice which echoed from the far ends of the street, and a laugh which rang out and sent the birds flying up from the trees. It was Peter, Simon Peter, the big fisherman:

"The big boat is Peter's, he could hardly get into a smaller one," was what Jesus had told her on her visit with him to Capernaum, and he was right. Peter had come to see Mary, the mother of his Master, Jesus. "Mary, Holy Mother, I come to salute you. Greatest of mothers, mother of the greatest of men…from the many thousands who throng to hear him, salutations, salutations and thanks." The whole house seemed to resound with the joyfulness of the big fisherman. He tried to kneel at Mary's feet but finding that he was too tall, or Mary too short, he swept her momentarily on high. "Rejoice, oh Galilee," he cried, "rejoice in the one who gave birth to our Saviour." He put her down again. He picked up the baby, and threw him high in the air. Abigail was alarmed. The baby, delighted, clutched at Peter's beard and chortled happily. Peter lifted great pieces of wood, and blessed them. "Blessed be the trees, made by our Lord in Heaven. Blessed be you, James, master of this house. Blessed be you, Joseph, wise artificer."

After the initial welcome, there was time for talking. Peter told them many things, confirmed some, and repudiated others. He said that it was a time of salvation. Happy were they who had been chosen to accompany Jesus. The harvest was ready, he and Jesus and the other disciples were there, and the gathering had begun. It would have been hard not to feel enthusiastic in the presence of Peter, and Mary would have been a sceptic indeed not to hope that what she was hearing foretold of a Galilee that would be a centre for a whole new world brought about by Jesus. If this was one of Jesus' new brothers, the Lord had been good. Peter finally left, the children of the area running along with him until approaching darkness drove them back to their homes.

Whether Peter had been sent by Jesus, Mary never questioned, nor indeed knew. He was the sort of person who would have done things on his own. She felt that this would be a person you would be glad to be with if things went wrong; she was surprised to find herself even contemplating "things going wrong"...it hardly seemed a possibility in the presence of the jovial and masterful Peter.

Mary found that she had forgotten to ask if Peter knew what was happening to her cousin John. John had not been, as they would have expected, one of the disciples. Was he in Jerusalem? Or had he gone to baptise or to preach repentance elsewhere? There was room for it in the cities of the Nile. She could imagine John crossing the desert to make for the east. Balthazar would have been at one with John. Peter with all his noisiness would have appreciated Melchior. She had always thought of Jesus as a friend of the youngest of the wise men. Now she thought of the third wise man as the youngest of Jesus' disciples.

The news that came drove away such happy thoughts and imaginings. It could have been palace spies that Joseph had noticed watching and listening to John beside the river. Herod Antippas, ruler and a sort of successor to the infamous Herod, had sent and had John arrested and put into prison. Herod Antippas, living with Herodias, wife to his own brother Philip, had plenty of need for repentance. John, unbowed, was likely to remain in prison. There were those who had started to say that Jesus ought to perform a miracle and lift John out of the palace dungeons.

It was at this time that the travels of Jesus through Galilee were becoming less happy. The nearer he came to Nazareth, the more did jealousy become apparent. They were not going to have a man like Jesus, a carpenter's son, telling them what to do, oh dear no. There were one or two potentially ugly scenes, and men would not listen to his message. The circumstances of his birth were recalled. There were those who whispered that even if he could give healing, who would want to be healed by a bastard? Mary's own character had the slightly unfair effect that people started saying that Jesus was the illegitimate son of Joseph…Mary, the kind and good, must keep the picture they had in their minds of a saint, and therefore a bride going to her husband as a virgin. Jesus though…they weren't going to listen to him. He had better clear out.

The disciples were being sent out by Jesus, to travel through the land, to heal, to spread his teaching. Had he hoped to establish some definite centre, here in Galilee, from which his teaching might spread, without conflict even with Jerusalem? His teaching was so very simple. Listen to the voice of God. Be as concerned for your neighbours as you are for yourself. He did not urge conflict with Caesar. He was not establishing a new outward kingdom. Perhaps Jesus, as well as Mary, had hoped that he might remain in Galilee, only to be repelled by a lack of faith as he drew near to Nazareth. Can a prophet ever be with honour in his own country? It must have been sadly that he found himself turned away.

The news then came of the execution of John, John their cousin, John who had become known as "John the Baptist". His death might have been easier to bear if there had been some sort of a trial, some semblance of an accusation that could have been answered. But to die at the whim of an idle girl and her wanton mother; Mary thought of the hopes that her mother's cousin Elizabeth had had when she was at last with child. John was to have been a greater man than Zachariah. Had the hope really come to naught? Or had the preaching of John prepared the way, as he had himself proclaimed, for one greater than himself? And was that one Jesus?

Two more disciples came to visit her, especially sent this time by Jesus. These were the brothers John and James, of the family of Zebedee, who lived by the lakeside in Capernaum. John was already becoming known as a specially loved disciple. He seemed to Mary to be a fine person, warm and loving, different from Peter in that Peter, also warm and loving, had seemed more triumphant, more to be one to act by himself. John and James spent the whole day with Mary and the family. Mary wondered if all James's were born to be good seconds to more brilliant elder brothers. This James, like hers, gave an impression of great reliability, and the two James's talked long together.

John talked to each of the family in turn, as, thought Mary, Jesus would have done. He did not throw Abigail's baby into the air, as Peter had done, but he did give Abigail some enchanting pieces of reed for him to play with, through one of which, it was later discovered, you could *blow* and get a noise. John asked Mary many questions, and heard many things about her own life and her husband's, and the early life of his master, Jesus. He was much more interested in hearing about Mary's husband… "Jesus had spoken of him so often, and of your father."

For Mary, talking with John was like talking with her own father. Surely no harm could befall if Jesus had such companions. She became more aware, as John talked, of the impact that Jesus was making. Presently she asked the question that had long been in her mind, but had not been spoken. How much danger was there for Jesus in what he was doing? John did not answer quickly. Finally, he acknowledged that there were dangers. There were the obvious ones, the sickness or accident that can happen. Jesus had as little to fear, perhaps less than most people, in that way. There was though another danger, not unlike that for his cousin John, and that was serious.

What Jesus was preaching was going to bring him enemies, had already brought him enemies. Some people had turned against him. He would not be able to stay in Galilee. There had already been the time when men had tried to seize him and actually throw him out of a town; an ugly situation, it had been. Jesus had not raised a finger…just walked calmly straight through the crowd. (This story of the escape of Jesus was always remembered by Mary. It did not seem to have made so much impression on others, though there was a Greek physician who got hold of the story, later on.) "Mary, holy Mother," said John, "I think God will keep your son's *life* safe until and unless the time comes when one of us lifts a hand in anger."

John fell silent. Mary thought about Peter, and presently John smiled and added, "Except for Peter of course. He does wrong things, often, but then he repents, and somehow no one would hold it against him. One day, not a month ago, someone jeered at the Master, and Peter threw the man into the lake; then he jumped in after him to save him, and nearly drowned. Jesus had to go in after them and save them both. We couldn't help laughing. But for the rest of us, apart from Peter, the life of Jesus can be forfeit if any one of us raises an angry hand." John went on, probably explaining things to himself as much as to Mary, "What it really comes to is this. Jesus isn't the only one of our Jewish people, and I pray will not be the last, to have had such a sense of God's purpose. Only Jesus *likes* everyone as well, and then he sees what everyone might become, as he has done with all of us, and urges everyone on to that. The secret, if there is one, is that he works through love and does not use force. I suppose that's why I say that he may be safe so long as none of us raises a hand in anger."

John finished his talk with Mary, and he and James left. Mary, thankful to have met and talked with John, would now face the truth…it was not going to be possible for Jesus to stay in Galilee, where his presence would only cause strife, strife between his own loving family and unbelieving neighbours. Her second hope was over; Jesus was about to leave Galilee.

Neither John nor Mary had then understood that it might be uncritical adulation from which Jesus was seeking escape.

26

Opposition from the Temple

THE FAMILY COULD hardly expect to see Jesus again until they met in Jerusalem at a Passover. Jesus himself and his disciples now left Galilee. They travelled up to Tyre and Sidon on the coast, there to continue the teaching, the healing, and the meeting with the many. Young Joseph often thought about them; he was finding increasing satisfaction in taking on more of the responsibility for the family business; he wondered how he would have fared with the disciples, and whether he would have understood what Jesus was actually doing. It must have been odd, he thought, for Jesus to have no proper home. Even a fox had its own lair. Mary could have explained that sometimes there were more important things than staying in one's own home.

Jesus and the disciples were credited with appearances far to the north; some said that they had been visiting Asia Minor, others that they had been seen at Ephesus or in Corinth. That they had *not* been in Ephesus or Corinth or even Asia Minor was ascertained when Rachel and Ephraim visited Nazareth. Rachel, now with a second child, and Ephraim had returned to live not very far away, in Caesarea Philippi. Rachel's looks still betokened outward strain, as well, it had to be admitted, as inner content. Ephraim was often absent...on affairs of business, said Rachel, who seemed happy enough in leading what to many Jewish wives would have been an impossibly lonely life. Mary wished that Rachel's many silences could have been construed as listening to the voice of God. She knew her daughter well, and was certain that whatever Rachel had in her mind, it was not the voice of their Lord, either as preached in the synagogue or as interpreted by Jesus and the disciples.

Mary's own visits to the Passover had been postponed. One year Esther and Samuel were awaiting their first child, and Mary was unwilling to be far away (it was a boy, healthy to judge from the noise he was soon making). The second year, it was Abigail who was with child. The baby was born in the summer months, was a daughter, and was called Naomi. Mary reminded Abigail how certain she had been that it would be a daughter, and Abigail laughed. She was the excellent wife and mother that she had been brought up to be, but living in the household that had once been that of Jesus of Nazareth had made her much less exacting in her demands. Mary reflected on the great difference between her older daughter and her daughter-in-law, and how good each was in her own special way. She did not think, as some might have been tempted to in her position, that Rachel should have been a more careful housewife, or Abigail a more imaginative parent. How good they each were.

In this she was reflecting, perhaps unwittingly, some of the lessons being preached by Jesus. Each day-labourer had been paid what had been agreed, ran one parable, so why be envious that the master of the vineyard had not given more to the man who had started work in the morning? Why be envious of the good fortune of others? If your own gift lies in cooking a fine dinner for the family and guests, as Abigail's did, why malign the sister who sits and listens, as Rachel would, to a guest who is uncovering some great truth? The lesson was handed down to future generations, though with different names, and not about Mary's own family.

Mary was much occupied with children, and with grandchildren, and always thinking about and praying for the absent Jesus. She mused on the fame that he had achieved; his words were often quoted, even in synagogues which had rejected him. His actions, and those of his disciples, were continually being reported. If it was strange to think of Levi, whom they remembered as a tax collector, now being the disciple Matthew, it was no less strange to think of men of learning listening to fisher folk like Peter and John and James. There were no more stories of towns driving them out, and Mary began to dream her third hope. Her third hope, as devastatingly simple as the teachings of Jesus, was that these teachings, so straightforward and direct, should be received, and that Jesus, without actually returning to them, would yet "settle down" somewhere, accepted by all, perhaps in Jerusalem. Isaiah's words would come true, and she remembered how her father had recited them; "The wolf shall also lie down with the lamb, and the leopard shall lie down with the kid, and the calf and the young lion and the fatling together, and a little child shall lead them…the earth shall be full of the knowledge of the Lord, as the waters cover the sea." The prophecy might not come true in the literal sense of the words, but now, here, surely, was there not the vision for which man had been waiting, of a people united and at peace, at one in spirit, together in true worship of one God and creator?

Mary's third hope, which was possibly that of Jesus as well, was not to be fulfilled. The stories that had not reached her were of the serious opposition to Jesus from the authorities of the Temple. When Jesus carried out a spectacular healing, the news spread. The carping of the Pharisees who might have been present was more difficult to report. The man whose son had been healed of epilepsy proclaimed it from the rooftops. The scribe who had failed to trap Jesus in some sophisticated argument went quietly back to his confederates. It was small wonder that news never reached Mary of the initial difficulties, and now of the increasing danger in which Jesus could find himself if he approached Jerusalem.

It was when the third Passover, after Jesus had left them, was getting near, that there was a visit from another of the disciples. It coincided, apparently by chance, with a visit from Rachel, accompanied on this occasion by her husband Ephraim. The disciple was the one called Judas;

he was always known as Judas Iscariot, to distinguish him from the many other people of the same name. For a moment, Mary had hoped that this meant the message from Jesus that he was "settling down". Judas took little notice of her, and none indeed of the children. He seemed to be a clever man, and he spent a great deal of the time talking with James as well as with Ephraim. Had Jesus really been planning to "settle down", these busy men might have been discussing the ways and means. Judas was heard to say to Ephraim that there were "many Gentiles too who are even now prepared to come in with us". He seemed to Mary to have less confidence than the other disciples that she had met. She looked at the lines on his anxious-looking face, and would have liked to take him by the hand and lead him away to some place where he could sit quietly and think. For no very clear reason, she knew that her third hope was vanishing. When Judas left, it was with the briefest of words of farewell, and the bald statement that "all" would be at the Passover. It was not clear if he meant that all the disciples would be there, or that some great event would take place.

This, the third Passover since Jesus left, was to be the one attended by Mary and the family. It was easier to leave woodwork than it had been to leave animals. She recalled the arrangements that had had to be made when she went on her first visit to the Passover, and how the years had passed between her first visit, with her father and her two brothers, and her second, with her husband Joseph and three small children, Jesus only seven years old. How Jesus had enjoyed that visit, and that first meeting with their cousin John. Now John was dead, executed at the wish of Herod Antippas, and Jesus was a man of importance. Now the time had gone—remarkable the events.

Jesus in fact had become a man of such importance that in Jerusalem the Scribes and the Pharisees were wondering how to react if he came to the Passover. His very presence now was a threat to them. "Jesus and his gang," they were thinking. The man was making too many people feel important…publicans, prostitutes and the like, rabble really. He was preaching for Gentiles as well as Jews. He was making some of their own laws and regulations look ridiculous; worse, when he was challenged in the open, his answers had the crowd on his side. "What, oh Master," a scribe would sneer, "what are the laws that you are proclaiming?"

"Worship the Lord thy God, honour thy father and thy mother," he had replied, and it was the scribe who was discomforted.

The whisperings in the Temple went on. Jesus, alone except perhaps for John, grew to realise that his life would be in jeopardy if they reached Jerusalem. All the same, they must make ready and come up to Jerusalem for this Passover.

27

A Den of Robbers

IN THIS, THE third year after Jesus had left, the family prepared to go up to the Passover. There were many in the party, family, friends, and neighbours. For Mary, although the time had come for the longed-for visit, it was with an unquiet spirit that she set out. There was the great and overriding hope that Jesus would be there, that she would see him again and talk with him, but as well as this, she felt an uneasy foreboding. After Judas visited them, she kept wondering why there had been no message from Jesus. Surely there should have been one? Or had Judas stolen away from the disciples without Jesus or any of them knowing? And if so, then why, what was happening? She tried to banish fear from her mind, a fear that was the more insidious in that it was for Jesus and not herself, and a fear of…she knew not what. *Festin alin*, as the children said, one must persevere; it was not easy.

It was a large party that went up to Jerusalem, so large that in fact any one of them could have slipped away unnoticed, everyone thinking that Joseph or Jesse or Mary or whoever was with someone else. Only the small children were shepherded, and that carefully, for there seemed an unusually large number of people on the way; indeed, as they approached Jerusalem, soldiers too were in evidence, with the air of men on the lookout for possible trouble. Someone heard one soldier swearing to another something about "Caiaphas stirring it up", the soldier adding a few descriptive words before the name. It seemed an odd thing to say; the only Caiaphas most of them knew of was the High Priest, who surely was the last one to want to stir up trouble at the time of the Passover?

Unknown to the party for some time was the fact that they were following the route taken by Jesus and the disciples. A considerable number of people had attached themselves to the disciples' party, and more were expecting them. As Jesus neared Jerusalem, an impromptu celebration broke out. Jesus was riding at the head of the group, and they were welcomed on all sides with shouts of "Hosanna" and a waving of torn-off branches. It was like a Roman triumph, except that there were no defeated. It was well for Mary that her own party was an hour's journey behind; it would have been bitter for her to have seen that tumultuous reception, and then experience what followed before the end of the Passover.

Mary's own party was presently halted. Their way ahead was blocked with piles of branches, and with people wandering about. Two soldiers, close to Mary, told them that it wouldn't be long. They looked hot and dusty. Mary offered them water from her own small store, and was greeted with a polite refusal, "Thank thee, Mother, we have our own." She wondered if all the soldiers were as good-natured as these? A more likely explanation was that soldiers did not expect a middle-aged woman pilgrim to be offering them water. The soldiers moved on ahead to where, judging from the noise, there was some sort of trouble. There were some shouts, and angry cries, and the wailing of children. Then came a commanding voice and a hush, and order was apparently restored.

What surprised Mary and those of her group within hearing, was that it was the voice of a *woman* that had echoed out so commandingly. Women's voices could be raised in woe, or in supplication, but a woman's voice in command? A clear, musical, compelling voice, the voice almost of a professional entertainer from Rome or some other great city, a voice accustomed to swaying an audience. When Mary's two soldiers were back beside the column, they explained. Yes, it was a woman who had told them all what to do, good thing too; that, they said, was Mary of Magdala. There was respect in their voices. Mary of Magdala, everyone knew, was the most famous courtesan of all Judea. "Not for the likes of us, oh Mother, but for the important ones, the captains and…and those even from your own community, Mother, provided they have money enough. *We* haven't." Mary's thoughts went back to Egypt, where many of the prostitutes she had known, friends of her neighbour's, were indeed entertainers. She remembered the presents they received, and some of the trinkets and scents that Vashti brought back from them, and the day that the five-year old Jesus had appeared garlanded with flowers and bedewed with perfume, as one being prepared to solicit on the streets. She asked the soldiers if Mary, who was of *Magdala*, was she not, often came to Jerusalem.

"No, Mother. The Magdalene is a Jew, brought up as a Jew, and sufficiently ashamed of her calling not to come to your festivals. But it's different this year. This Jesus, who's not far in front of us, had converted her. That's what people are saying; quite a feather in his cap, if he has. Mind you, the poor devil is going to need all his friends if he's got the Temple lot against him. That lot won't have liked it if what our mates told us did happen…that the people up in front had lined up and shouted Hosanna as Jesus went in."

The soldiers were ordered to press forward, and called out goodbye; "Take care, Mother, there are rogues about but it's not far and then you can have a rest."

Mary did not feel it was a rest she needed. What was important was to get to Jerusalem. She prayed to herself for the safety of Jesus. She hoped more and more that she would see him and actually be with him. She remembered that long-ago first approach to Jerusalem and the dying man. What had been her prayer then? That she might be ready to hear and to obey the word of God? She had felt more certain then that there would be something that she could do. Now she was powerless. It was an effort to hold back her tears…but one must be ready in case there was something one was called on to do.

As they arrived in Jerusalem, the party was divided up. Some trouble or disorder had already occurred, and the soldiers had been ordered to keep the people in small groups. As some of Mary's companions protested, the clear voice of the Magdalene was heard: "Mary, holy Mother, the soldiers are only doing their duty, we should do as they say." Mary turned with pleasure to greet the Magdalene, this fine woman who was a friend of her son's. For a few moments, the two women were together. When the Magdalene left (she went to find out how the disciples were faring), Mary found that she had been parted from the rest of her company and was alone in the crowd. She picked up the news that was going from one to another...the Temple has been plundered...the money-changers have been turned out...the outer courts are in ruin...it was a Nazarene...it was not a Nazarene...the extortionists and the grasping have been thrown out into outer darkness, with wailing and gnashing of teeth. Mary was carried along with the crowd to the edge of the Temple precincts. After a momentary look at the scene of destruction, most of the people surged on to find each his own lodging place for the coming night. The destruction was largely superficial, but to see even that in the precincts of the Temple was bad enough. People took one horrified look and hurried away.

It was here, with the afternoon light dim behind the piles of broken tables, that Mary was to have her last meeting with Jesus before—before what happened.

She looked around, uncomprehendingly, at a scene that

seemed of ill-omen for the coming festival. Then she heard and went to help a weeping child. He was crouched down holding a badly "hurted" dove which, he explained between his sobs, had been intended specially for a sacrifice. The pigeon was badly hurt; Mary firmly ended the bird's life. The bird, said the boy, had been hurt when that angry man, one of the Nazarenes, who usually *help* people…had thrown the tables about. Did the lady think that the sacrifice would count now? Yes, the lady thought that if you had done your duty (which she was sure he had) then the sacrifice would be accepted. Things didn't always turn out as you expected, but you went on doing your best and the best thing that he could do now would be to go and find his mother, who might be worrying about him. The boy departed, whistling cheerfully. She was a nice lady, he thought, nicer than that angry man had been. Mary was left wondering which of the disciples had been that angry man. Peter?

Suddenly, Jesus was beside her. He had been searching for her. For a few moments, there was the gladness of being together. Mary, holy Mother; Jesus, my son. The afternoon light was fading, the precinct emptying. Jesus and Mary could talk on without interruption. There was much to say, so much to ask.

Mary voiced her immediate question. This was the action of your big disciple, Peter? She listened aghast to the answer. It was Jesus himself who had done this. She thought of the "hurted" dove. This work of destruction, it could not be right. Appalled, she remembered the words that the loving disciple John had said to her, "If one of us raises a hand in anger, the life of Jesus will be forfeit."

Then she became once more a mother ready to chide a son for a wrong action. Quite apart from any consideration of what the results might be, what Jesus had done was *wrong*. Could there be an explanation? She asked Jesus why he had done this.

The answer was not short, and took the form of one of Jesus' stories. There was a certain man, he said, who was assailed by three winged dragons. The first dragon, he said, was fear, and the man defeated him by always looking him straight in the face. The second dragon, who came sneaking up from behind, was pride. The voice of Jesus faltered, "Oh, Mary, holy Mother," he cried in anguish, "*I* am that certain man. Pride might have overcome me, for I was able to help many people, but their love and thanks drove away all thought of pride. You should have seen them, oh Mother (perhaps in your mind's eye, you did), the lunatic restored to health, the prostitute to self-respect, the tax gatherer as a helper and not an oppressor...the whole world of the poor and outcast being redeemed, the Jew and the Gentile at peace. It was fine, fine. The vision was being achieved, the earth was the Lord's, and everyone's love and reverence defeated the winged dragon of pride. It was after this that the third dragon came stalking in, that dragon whose name was righteous anger. When I entered this Temple, to look on what might be the centre for a whole new world, and I saw a den of robbers, then the third dragon overcame me. With my own hands, I flung out those whom I thought evil-doers and I hurled down their tables." Jesus ended with the great cry of despair, "My God, my God, why didst Thou forsake me?"

If Mary had been a storyteller, she would have couched her rebuke as the end of the story, reminding Jesus that there were four dragons, not three. He had forgotten despair. This was the dragon that he must now face. As a mother, talking to a child who has been wayward, she firmly reminded him of the rest of the Psalm. It was well to quote, "My God, my God, why hast thou forsaken me?" as indeed her own father had had occasion to, but, after that, one went on to the rest of the Psalm. Although the opening verses were of sadness, Jesus must now join her as they recited the rest together. Mary led the reciting, gravely repeating verse after verse, until Jesus too joined in. It was his voice that led the triumphant; "For the kingdom is the Lord's and he is the governor among the nations." His mother had uttered a fitting rebuke. Whatever might now happen, he was ready to face it.

He must now prepare her. The future for him, he said, was bleak. It would now be arrest, beating, imprisonment, even death. Had he been a Roman, he would have been considering whether to take his own life. This a Jew does not do. The great future, for which he had begun to hope, must now rest with, at first, the little band of the twelve. The voice of Jesus was quite calm now, quite clear. "Mary, holy Mother, not each of them has a parent who had known when to chide and when to encourage. There is one, I think, who may need your help to overcome despair." Mary at once thought of Judas. She wished she could have been sure that when Jesus had to die, whenever that was, it would be with the assurance that not one of the twelve had failed him. This would be her prayer. Perhaps this was what God wanted her to do.

Then, as if that subject had been disposed of, Jesus turned to the family, and asked for news in the manner of a son who has been working away from home. For just that little while, they allowed themselves to be any happy mother and son waiting for the Passover to begin and filling in the time with the glad exchange of tidings. Jesus asked particularly about Abigail and about Joseph. It was good that Abigail was so capable, for there might be wider work for James, while clever young Joseph could have a life's work as a carpenter of Nazareth. Mary asked about the different disciples, and had her opinion of John confirmed.

Darkness was falling. The time for the farewell was coming. Mary knew the way to her lodgings? Indeed, yes. Ought he to warn her more specifically that his own death could be near? He thought she knew. Ought he to tell her which of the disciples might be expected to falter? It would be better for her not to think about it too much beforehand. Was there anything that she might have wanted to ask him in the past and not had an opportunity? He remembered, unexpectedly, that he had never explained to his mother the reasons, when he had been twelve years old, that he had had for staying on at the Passover. "Ro-li-ma," he said, and the question at once sounded casual, happy, confident, "is there anything thee would ask me?"

Mary thought. Yes, there was one thing. The nickname "Rolima" had reminded her. "Jesus, my son, tell me. Did you ever promise that you would marry Vashti?"

Jesus was nonplussed. Marry Vashti? Vashti, the word used to describe an uproar. Then he remembered the cries of a nine-year-old little girl, as his family and two donkeys started the journey back from Egypt. She had shouted out, "You mustn't marry anybody else." He put his head back and laughed and laughed. No, Mother, he had not promised. He embraced his mother and left. Their time had gone. It was a good present that she had given him, the last laugh in his life.

When Mary left the Temple, it was to find the Magdalene waiting to conduct her to her lodgings. The Magdalene, like everyone else in the city by then, had heard the rumours about what might happen to Jesus. As she had friends in high places, she knew that on this occasion the rumours were only too true. She was now trying desperately to do what she could to save the life of the man whose vision had transformed her own life. She had hoped that Nicodemus, a man of importance now in the Temple, might be able to help her, but somehow Nicodemus was not to be found. It seemed that there was little that they, the women, could do that night. There was one woman in Jerusalem who might help, and that was the wife of Pontius Pilate, the Roman governor; it was said that she had met Jesus and been impressed. They must hope.

28

The Crucifixion

IT WAS THE next morning when the family heard the news. The news was as bad as it could be. Jesus had been arrested, in the Garden of Gethsemane. His disciples had fled. If that was not bad enough, there was, for Mary, something even more wretched to try to comprehend. It was that *Judas* had led the Temple's gang out to the Garden to find and arrest Jesus. It was the work of Judas, one of the very twelve, one who had sat with Jesus at their supper together, the last supper before his arrest. The scribes and the Pharisees, that lot from the Temple, had been set to get Jesus. Possibly they could have picked him up in the streets, but then there would have been the crowd to contend with. And Judas—*Judas*—had taken them to where Jesus was with some of his disciples, praying in the Garden. Some of the disciples had been sleeping too.

It was true. Jesus had had the evening meal, the one for the eve of the Passover, alone with his disciples. He had warned them of what was coming. He had made a solemn ceremony of breaking the bread and drinking the wine. These ordinary actions of every day, these they must always do in remembrance of him. He was their leader, whom they loved, and they had been ready to do as he said, each in turn faithfully pledging his own life. Master, each thought in his inmost being, I will serve to the end. But one had failed. Judas, clever lonely Judas, had himself led the Temple's minions out to where Jesus was praying.

Jesus was now in custody. The Sanhedrin had spent the night with jeering and accusations. They had found some trumped-up charge, and managed to have Jesus sent off, bruised and bloodstained, to appear before the Roman governor.

This much was faithfully retailed to Mary and the family by the Magdalene. What was happening, now that Jesus was before Pilate, not even the Magdalene could find out. They could only watch and pray. This was what the disciples were doing. For John and James, there was the bitter memory that they had not stayed awake in the Garden of Gethsemane, that they had left Jesus without human fellowship when they could have given it. Now, was it too late? If only they had known that it might be the last hour that they could spend with their living master. They knelt and prayed. Peter should have been there too, but was not.

Judas was not with them, and nor was he with the people to whom he had betrayed his master. Who knew what fantasy had been in his mind? Had he dreamt of Jesus leading an armed riot? He brought back the thirty pieces of silver he had received, went out, and—Jew though he was—hanged himself. He left to posterity a name that in the future would be synonymous with "traitor". Mary prayed that this news at least, of the death of Judas, might not reach Jesus.

Jesus, now a political prisoner, was sent to appear before Pontius Pilate. Little of what happened there was revealed to his friends. They were still praying for a miracle that would deliver him back to them. That he was scourged for a start was of course known, and some said later that Pilate would have liked to end the matter there. That Jesus was knocked about, treated with every possible insult—that was what happened to a prisoner whose friends were the humble, whose enemies the mighty of the land. Most prisoners in that state tried to ingratiate themselves with the soldiery, making promises and vain offers of what their friends would do. Jesus remained silent. The captain of the guard had begun to think that they were doing someone else's dirty work for them—this man, grievously hurt, and in addition having been betrayed by one of his closest followers, was yet bearing it with dignity. Not that that was going to help him much, if the Temple was out for his death. The captain would have liked it all over.

A young soldier came rushing in, eager to taunt Jesus with the news that Judas had hanged himself. He received an ugly slap across the mouth from the captain. No need for the poor devil of a prisoner to know that. Word of the dramatic event passed quietly round the soldiers. That it was withheld from Jesus was one of the last acts of kindness he would receive.

Mary and the disciples—half Jerusalem—waited. Pontius Pilate was coming to the opinion that the prisoner was innocent. He was about to follow the custom of releasing one prisoner. Jesus or Barabbas? Which one would be the question, though he guessed only too well the answer. Temple agents knew their work, and there would be plenty ready to shout "Barabbas". Pilate would have liked to save Jesus of course; however, he would put the question and he washed his hands of the result. The answering roar "Barabbas" reached Mary, the disciples, the Magdalene, the family. Then, as Jesus was paraded, came the cries of, "Crucify, crucify" from the well-prepared in the crowd.

The centurion and some of the soldiers loaded the heavy crosses, two on condemned thieves, one on the half-fainting form of Jesus. The centurion pointed to a burly man in the waiting crowd, who found himself hauled out to carry the third cross. The centurion was doing what he could for this prisoner. He did not dare to take off the derisory crown with the words: "King of the Jews".

Whatever the mood of the crowd, sympathy with Jesus was growing among the soldiers whose job it was to manage the events of the afternoon. The captain who was in charge at the place for the execution allowed some of the disciples to gather near, and even Mary too and another woman.

After a long wait, the two condemned thieves appeared, followed by Jesus. Mary saw that he was at the end of his strength, as someone else was carrying his cross. It was a big man, and was probably Peter, who had not been with the disciples. She fell to her knees and prayed. It was no longer a prayer that the life of Jesus should be spared. It was a prayer that they, his helpers, should be strong enough to show that his work would go on, to show this to the crowd, to show it to the man who would be dying on the cross.

The captain became aware that a woman, apparently of importance, was moving up through the crowd. He remembered the rumour that Pilate's wife was a friend of this Jesus. Well, this would be just what was wanted to complete an appallingly ugly situation, the crowd ready to be unruly, the Temple wanting one thing, Pilate another, feelings running high, the Jews themselves divided. He ordered the soldiers to clear a path for the woman; better not take any chances. He was horrified when the woman emerged, and he saw that it was no Roman lady, but the Magdalene. He swore that the harlot of Magdala should not appear, reformed sinner or not, to start some performance here. Mary raised a gentle hand to his arm. "She has befriended my son," she said, and the Magdalene stayed.

In silence, in a hideous silence, the two thieves, then Jesus, were nailed to the crosses, and the crosses raised. Time passed. A few raucous voices called out insults. Then one thief called out from his cross that if Jesus was that bloody powerful, he should show it by rescuing them. The second thief called out too, using the last of his strength to make his voice carry out over the crowd. He cried out that *they* were guilty and deserved to die, but not Jesus…this man…here…Jesus is a *good man, he is innocent*. The words rang out, and the mood of the crowd began to change as they remembered the many fine acts of Jesus.

Mary had no idea how long the silence lasted, or how often it was interrupted. She was praying to be ready if called upon. Jesus started to say something. She rose to her feet. She listened intently. She must know what he *meant* as well as what he might manage to say. It was the opening words of the twenty-second Psalm, "My God, my God, why hast Thou forsaken me?" She knew what she had to do. She must carry on reciting the words of the Psalm, with Jesus, or—as his strength failed—without him. Her voice carried a little way. John joined in. Mary got as far as, "they divide my garments among them", before her voice failed. Another, more carrying voice, joined in. It was the Magdalene. Together, she and John, the loved disciple, recited the verses. Then John's voice too faltered. The Magdalene, with the tears pouring down her face, kept on to the end, the practised voice of the entertainer ringing out loud and clear. "For the kingdom is the Lord's, and he is governor among the nations." It was the biggest audience she had ever had, and she was speaking to one dying man.

The end came sooner than the soldiers had expected. They started to haul down the cross on which hung the unmoving body of Jesus. Mary, almost unconscious, was carried away by John and the Magdalene. They were escorted through the crowd by two ashen-faced Roman soldiers.

Mary was taken back to the lodgings. Of the events immediately after the Crucifixion, she apprehended little. She thought and hoped that Jesus had somehow known that they had kept on reciting the whole psalm, and that this was in earnest that his work would go on, that he was not dying in vain. There was nothing more for her to do. She had an impression that there had been great noise and clamour, but could not have said if this had been some awe-inspiring natural phenomenon or her own imagination.

29

The Journey Home

FOR JAMES AND Abigail, the important task would now be to get Mary home. That the end of the journey for Mary might be death—that was at once in Abigail's mind. Might that not be a mercy? Mercy or not, the immediate task was to get Mary out of Jerusalem.

Few could have said how the little family emerged from that crowd. Hardly aware of what was happening, they were guided to the outskirts of the crowd. Initial resentment at the presence of the soldiers gave place to stunned acceptance. Long afterwards, Abigail could still see in her mind's eye the figures of Roman soldiers bearing an unconscious Mary.

Somehow...later...a day later?...days later?...they found themselves on the well-known road heading for the north. Somehow, Rachel was there too. Their own little party was not the only one travelling in anxiety and grief. On all sides was unrest. Those less burdened passed them, pausing for the briefest of greetings. Lacking was the happy sharing of memories and impressions that usually marked the return from the Passover.

James at times had the impression that there were soldiers intent on escorting his little group home. It was to Rachel that the situation was explicable. Authority wanted Mary and her family out of the way or at least out of Jerusalem, and authority was seeing to it. The soldiers were under orders to escort them to Nazareth and would carry out those orders, just as other soldiers, long ago, had gone to kill babies in Bethlehem.

The officers were on horseback. It was the presence of one of the horses that set off the...the metamorphosis...of the next three days. An officer was riding near the litter that had been provided for Mary. He looked down at her and felt strangely moved. Mary roused herself and quite calmly asked, "What is your horse called?" To Abigail the question would have been quite incomprehensible, but she was not re-living earlier days as Mary was, and was not hearing the excited voice of a small boy, "Mummy, Grandpa says that you once rode on a Roman horse. Was it a brown horse? Mummy, you never told us about it, what was it called? Did an angel tell it what to do?"

Just as an earlier officer years ago had responded to the intrinsic goodness of Mary, this one became aware that he must—not just do his duty, but try to give help. He called one of his men over, and they told Mary what the horse's name was and explained what it had come from. Mary all at once seemed alive again. She thanked them, and started asking the soldier where he came from, and did he have a wife, and had they any children? She slipped out of the litter and stood up, ready to walk. Her clear voice was that of a more youthful Mary.

The soldiers motioned Rachel to approach. The party moved on. Mary's eyes rested on a nine-year old girl, with straight black hair, actually a niece of Rachel's husband. "Hallo, Vashti," Mary called out, "look, we've got a horse to talk to today, not just a little cat. The girl, though surprised, managed to say enough to play the part of someone called Vashti. Later on, Rachel would tell her who Vashti had been.

Mary talked to one and another, and for three days, each in turn tried, with some success, to give her help and assurance.

At a place where the road became difficult, Mary started to sing. "You should have been with us," she told whoever was next to her. "My father had a lovely voice. It was good to sing on the way to the Passover. But of course, we are coming back now." For a moment, a shadow seemed to cross her face.

They passed near some sheep. Mary called the little girl over. "Rachel, my dear," (so she was Rachel now) "I believe this is the very place where, when you were quite little, the boys pretended you were Jezebel, and you cried because you thought they were going to throw you to the dogs, but you can see they are only sheep. Not even a ram among them, like my Jacob."

Mary stopped still. As the others gathered round, she

reminded them that they, the strong and powerful, must ever look after the young and the frail. "Are we not all needing a shepherd?"

The evening meal on the last day was one that all (all that is except Mary) would remember for the rest of their lives. The soldiers had drawn to one side. Perhaps it was the place where Mary and her father had once drawn different families together. "Joseph," said Mary, addressing James, "will you speak the evening prayer, and then we will share our meal?" She looked round. "Where is Jesus?" she asked. A little shiver went round, and then she answered herself: "Ah, gone with John and Elizabeth, I expect." James moved over beside her. He remembered how his father had prayed, and his grandfather, and Jesus. He raised his hand. Silence fell. The soldiers stopped checking their equipment. An officer took off his helmet and stood with head bent. James pronounced the words he had heard his father use, and, just as on that day long ago, all shared what they had.

For all, it would be a period that would stand out. Perhaps it was seldom that any of them spent an entire three days thinking only of how you help someone else.

They were approaching Nazareth, and the figure of "young" Joseph could be seen coming to meet them. Rachel, watching Mary, saw the youthfulness vanish away. It was a sad-eyed Mary who greeted her son. "Ah, Joseph, it is you who are the carpenter of Nazareth now."

30

Resurrection

MARY RECOVERED HER bodily strength, but with little will to do anything. She spent time just sitting and thinking, and remembering. She was thankful that she had understood what Jesus had tried to say on the cross. That, she thought, had been the last piece of work she could do for him. Thoughts of him would be ever with her, and she would sit and reflect.

Then came the morning when "an important visitor" was announced. She prepared to give the calm and resigned attention that was all she could muster these days. When the "important visitor" turned out to be just Rachel, even Mary smiled. "Rolima," said Rachel, "I told them to tell you it was someone important."

Mary's attention was roused. It was true that Rachel

seemed to hear things that other people didn't. Rachel explained: "The disciples of Jesus are here, in Galilee. They are waiting for something, but they do not know what. What has happened in Jerusalem, after the execution of Jesus, is not what the Temple intended. It is not a stop, not an end. The Pharisees have not achieved what they set out to do. Everyone is still talking about Jesus. And now, now, is the time when the disciples must come and give a lead. The harvest is ready." Rachel looked appraisingly at her mother. Mary's attention had been caught. Most people were trying to spare Mary any strain or effort, but it was not like Mary to sit with hands folded. There was work for her to do. Rachel tried to think of how Jesus would have acted. She could have wept as she remembered how she had herself refused to listen to one of his stories, the one about the bridesmaids. Well, she had chosen to be the bride, and she was now the one who had to convince Mary.

She explained to Mary that there were many people who were now ready to follow the way of Jesus, but the disciples must give the lead—the harvest was ready. It was no use saying they had seen the risen Christ unless they were prepared to go out and preach his message and only person who would make them do that was Mary. "Yes," said Rachel, "you, you Ro-li-ma, *festin alin*." Rachel paused, and left. She hoped she had said enough.

She had said enough. Mary was roused again, and ready to accept that the disciples must be told. She at once thought of Peter. It was Peter who had seemed the one to become leader. He was in Galilee and he came at her summons.

She looked with some alarm at his woebegone figure. He was as big as he had been, and yet he seemed so shrunken, a man bowed down under a burden unseen by others. Was this a man to give a lead? She thought of the last sight she thought she had had of him, carrying his Master's cross, just before she had herself fallen to her knees. So now she started by thanking him for his action.

It was this that broke through his reserve. He fell and wept, and hardly coherent, poured out to Mary the whole story.

After the supper, the last (his voice broke) they were to have with Jesus, they had gone to the Garden of Olives, and then, then, when Jesus had wanted them to stay awake with him, he had been one who slept. Slept. *Slept*, when they might have…he had failed, failed. And again after that, when he had gone along behind the people who had arrested Jesus… . He had gone to see if he could help in some way…and then, when someone asked him, he said he was not one of the Nazarenes…three times, three times he had said it…not one of them.

Peter paused. Mary sat quietly, but alert. The very acknowledgment of his failure seemed to have eased Peter. The burden was becoming bearable. He had not spoken of this before, perhaps because there was no one to listen. He went on talking, At the crucifixion, he said—far from being where he might have carried the cross, he had not dared to come nearer than the back of the crowd. He had heard the thief call out that Jesus was innocent; that had been a good action. He was not near enough to hear properly what happened after that, and he had heard two quite different stories of what his Master's last words had been; one that he had despaired, one that he had entrusted his spirit to God. Would Mary please tell him which was right? Mary answered. In a way, both the things he had heard were right, but it was the man who said Jesus was entrusting his spirit to God who had understood. The other words were despairing, but only when you realised that Jesus had not finished. Earlier, Jesus had said the whole Psalm through with her; on the cross he had said the opening verse, and then his strength had failed, and she and John had gone on a bit but it was the Magdalene alone who had gone on to the end. It was a triumph, not despair. It was a promise that the work Jesus had started should be continued.

Peter rose to his feet. He had had his question answered and he was a man with work to do. Mary of Magdala should not be the only one to go on to the end.

The next morning, the disciples were on their way back to Jerusalem.

Requiem

JAMES BECAME A follower of the disciples of Jesus, and went with Abigail and their family, to play a part in the new group in Jerusalem—a new church needed men of affairs as well as prophets.

For a while Mary lived on in Nazareth, where "young" Joseph had become the carpenter of Galilee. Some said that the spirit of Jesus was still there, and that it was because of Mary. For Mary herself, there was a different assurance—the spirit of Jesus was everywhere where men carried out his work, feeding the hungry, caring for those sick in mind as well as body, freeing those imprisoned by chains or by their own thoughts of evil. Might the will of God remain as clear to her as it had been among the hills in her childhood.

Finally, she went to live in the home of John, the beloved disciple. Her last days were spent there in Capernaum, where Jesus had once walked beside the sea on a sunlit afternoon.